'I believe I w
you,' Leonie sa
meant to show
alive.'

Jacques lifted his head and looked at Leonie the way no man had ever looked at her before. His gaze roamed all over her, making her feel exposed and desired.

He stepped forward, took hold of her shoulders, and lightly touched his lips to hers. He kissed her with all the passion she could have wanted. As his mouth drifted over hers all the questions she'd asked herself, all the debates she'd been having with herself, the constant back-and-forth, should-she-shouldn't-she? ended in that one exhilarating moment.

He gathered her into his arms and she sank into him, savouring his taste, inhaling his warm, masculine scent, feeling the heat of his body the strength of his arms encircling her. His ked into life parts of her that had been for a very, very long time.

Dear Reader

If you'd had one sweetheart for your entire adult life—from high school to raising a family and building a business, through illness and finally his death—and you'd never had a moment's doubt that he was the love of your life, what would you think were the chances of falling in love again?

No chance at all? That's what Leonie thinks too.

Falling in love for the second time after thirty years with one man is scary. It's like going skydiving again after crashing into the ground the first time. It takes courage, but it's exciting, and it can be surprising…

Falling in love is fabulous—at any age.

Best wishes

Claire

HER MEDITERRANEAN MAKEOVER

BY
CLAIRE BAXTER

For my mother, with love.

CHAPTER ONE

IT WAS so good to hear her daughter's voice. Leonie cradled the phone against her ear and wondered what she'd been thinking when she'd enrolled in a course on the other side of the world.

Yes, her children were legally adults, but they still needed her. And she needed them too. She'd never been separated from them before. Not for this long. No longer than a school camp, really.

'You could have sent me a text message, Mum. You didn't have to ring me again.'

'I just wanted to check that you'd worked out how to operate the washing machine. It's tricky if you're not used to it.'

'Yes, Mum. Your instructions were spot on.' Sam hesitated, then asked, 'Is that the real reason you called, Mum?'

'Of course!' Leonie winced at the fib. Samantha had always been the sensitive one. Even as a toddler she'd had the ability to pick up on her mother's moods. 'Well, to be honest, darling, I just wanted to make sure you were all right.'

'Yes, Mum, I'm all right. You don't need to worry.' Sam stressed the last few words.

'And your brother?'

'Kyle's fine too. Well, he's as obnoxious as ever, but we'll manage till you get home. It's only a matter of weeks, after all. This is *your* time, Mum, and you deserve it. Enjoy it.'

Easier said than done.

'It's not a matter of weeks, it's nearly *three months*! That's what a trimester means.'

'And there's only four weeks in a month,' Sam said, laughing. 'It will fly by. That's what you used to tell me when I didn't want to go back to school after the holidays, remember?'

She remembered. Oh, yes, she remembered. If only she could have that time over again. Fighting back tears as she said goodbye, Leonie clicked off the call, then went to the wide-open French doors that led to the single-person balcony of her one-room apartment. She couldn't see much of Nice, only the buildings across the narrow street. That was her fault for choosing to stay in the old town instead of a modern apartment in the city.

She'd rejected the idea of living in the residences at the language school just outside Nice, in favour of renting her own furnished apartment, figuring it would make for easy sightseeing. But she wasn't sure now that she'd made the right choice.

The apartment was so much smaller than it had looked on the internet. She'd thought it would be quaint, and it was, but to someone who was used to a spacious family home on a generous block of land in suburban Australia this apartment, with its kitchenette in one corner and a tiny shower off the main room, was quite a shock. As was the local custom of hanging washing on poles outside the window. She wasn't at all keen on displaying her underwear for passers-by to inspect.

There were times, like now, when this apartment made her feel claustrophobic, and she'd never experienced such a sensation in her life. Thank goodness for the balcony.

As usual, a petite old lady sat on the balcony that faced hers. She was always well groomed, and well dressed. Leonie wondered why she never went out. Was she waiting for someone who never came?

She'd tried smiling and waving at her, but received no reaction. Today she called out, *'Bonjour, Madame.'*

She received a cool nod. A slight advance on nothing.

Leonie looked along the street, wondering what to do to pass the time. She decided against sightseeing. Not that she didn't want to see the city, but she wasn't feeling up to doing it on her own. She'd tried to explore, but even with a guidebook she kept getting lost. Navigating had never been her strong point, but then she'd never really had to do it. On trips, her job had been to make sure every member of the family had enough to eat and drink, wore sunscreen and had a good time.

But now, her role had changed. Trouble was, when she did find the place she'd set out for, it brought home the realisation that she had nobody to share it with.

No husband and no kids. For so long, they'd been her whole life. It was disorientating to be alone like this.

Apart from missing her children like crazy, Leonie was not at all sure she'd done the right thing in taking on this language immersion course. It had seemed like a no-brainer when she'd first come up with the idea. She'd always wanted to improve her limited knowledge of French and she'd always wanted to travel, but what with marrying Shane straight out of high school, helping him build his business, then nursing him through his long illness while raising their children, she'd managed neither.

Now, three years after Shane's death, with both children at university, she was finally ready to find out for herself what the wider world had to offer, and she could afford to do it too. Between Shane's life insurance and the sale of his plumbing business, he'd left her very comfortably off. She'd never need to work.

Learning French in France…well, it had seemed like the perfect plan, but it hadn't turned out quite as she'd expected. For one thing, this language was really hard to learn. Or maybe she was too old for it. That saying about old dogs and new tricks was probably a cliché because it was true.

Either way, she was having a tough time making sense of what people were saying. The other students didn't seem to have the same problem, though, and she felt like a dill alongside them.

And that was another thing. She'd thought she'd make new friends on the course, but she hadn't counted on all the other students being so *young*. They were friendly enough, but when they asked if she'd like to go for a drink with them, they were only being polite. She could tell by the way they looked over her shoulder, careful not to make eye contact when they invited her.

So she didn't go. She didn't really want to anyway. It would be like socialising with her kids' friends, and wouldn't feel right.

She'd found the French people she'd met so far to be very polite. Shopkeepers went out of their way to greet her when she entered a store, which was nice, but in general they didn't seem to do conversation. Not with strangers anyway. Back home people would snatch any chance for a chat, but here, in her experience, the locals didn't speak unless spoken to, and then only reluctantly.

Except for the man who ran the little café she'd found the week before. She'd been wandering the narrow streets of old Nice—alleys, really, they weren't wide enough to be called streets—when an inconspicuous door had opened beside her, and the aroma that had poured out, combined with the sound of cheerful voices, had made her want to enter.

She'd looked up at the wall above the arched doorway but had seen no sign, only a brightly planted window box at a green-shuttered upstairs window. Still, the scent of strong coffee along with the sight of tiny round tables crammed into the small space had called to her like the Pied Piper's flute, and she'd followed it obediently. Inside she'd found a little café, and a welcome that had revived her as much as the coffee.

Jean-Claude, the elderly man who'd served her, had been friendly, chatty and interested in her. That alone would have been sufficient to bring her back, but she'd also enjoyed the ambience of jazz music playing softly from unconcealed speakers

on whitewashed walls alongside art that to her un-
educated eyes, looked ancient.

All the French newspapers were provided for
customers to read, and she'd enjoyed a lazy
browse, lingering over the few stories that she
could almost understand. If she was going to stay,
she thought now, it would be a good idea to set
herself the goal of figuring out more written
French each day.

Within minutes, she was out of the apartment
and heading for the café. She could go and buy
the papers for herself, but this was much nicer. It
allowed her the illusion that she was settling in.

Besides, it gave her something to do and she
needed that. During all those years of caring for
others, of being constantly busy, she'd dreamed
of taking a holiday alone, of having the time to
do nothing at all. But now that she had her wish,
she really wasn't sure that she liked it. Maybe
she'd just grown used to being needed, and here
no one needed her at all. It was an odd sensation.

The café was busy and Jean-Claude didn't have
time for chit-chat, and when she reached the newspaper rack only the most difficult one was left.
Well, difficult for her, she admitted as she tucked
it under her arm and carried her coffee to a table
at the back of the room. Understanding one word
in twenty did not make for an entertaining read.

Having spread the newspaper on the table, she took a sip of coffee and scanned the room, wondering if this was the norm and she'd just happened to turn up last week on the one day when the café was light on customers. As her gaze drifted from table to table she did a double take. A good-looking man was smiling at her. She glanced behind her, but no, there was no one standing there. Gosh, he really was smiling at *her*.

She smiled back. She'd seen him before. The first day she'd entered the café he'd been seated at the counter on one of the high stools. She couldn't help noticing him. Well, he did stand out in his pristine white shirt and dark trousers when most of the other patrons wore smart-casual clothes; her guess was that he worked nearby. But it was more than that—there was something about him that made *him* stand out…a presence. Charisma, was that it?

Whatever it was, he was still watching her. Maybe he thought he knew her from somewhere. If so, he was mistaken. With a mental shrug, she put down her coffee, reached into her handbag for her reading glasses and tried to concentrate on the words in front of her.

She was reasonably successful, despite being forced to glance up every few seconds to see whether he was still there. After a while, Leonie gave herself strict instructions not to look up for any reason at all until she'd read to the end of one full story. The shortest one would do.

Halfway through, though, she was interrupted by a male voice. When she looked over the top of her glasses, the man standing in front of her came into focus. The man who'd been smiling at her earlier. The same man she'd been unable to take her eyes off. And he was even better-looking close up.

Older than he'd appeared at first, he had just enough silver sprinkled through his hair to make him appear…safe. Same deal with the laughter lines around brown eyes that were so full of warmth and humour she found herself smiling even though she had no clue what he'd said.

She hurriedly shoved her glasses to the top of her head where they were anchored by her curly hair, then asked him to repeat his words. She watched his mouth closely as he spoke, trying her hardest to separate the sounds into individual words. Without much luck.

She shook her head and gave him an apologetic shrug.

Compassion filled his face and he leaned forward. *'Vous êtes sourde?'* he enunciated clearly.

Sourde, sourde… Leonie searched her memory for the word.

He covered his ears with his hands, following the action with a questioning lift of his eyebrows.

Deaf! That was it.

'Oh, my, no.' She shook her head. 'I'm from Australia.'

'I'm sorry,' he said, changing smoothly to English and smiling again. 'I didn't think of that. This café does not normally attract tourists.'

'I'm not surprised. It was pure chance that I found it. There's nothing outside to indicate that it is a café.'

'No. That's the way we like it.' He grinned. 'I'm sorry. I meant no offence.'

'Oh, none taken. I'm not a tourist.'

'*Ah, bon?* You live here?'

'Well, temporarily. I'm here to study the language so I'm a student. I look far too old to be one of those, I know. Do you object to students as well?' She smiled, sure that someone with eyes that gleamed with humour couldn't possibly be serious about disliking any group of people.

'Not at all. Nor do I object to tourists,' he said firmly. 'They are important to the economy, they create many jobs, so how could I?' He indicated the chair opposite her. 'May I?'

'Oh, yes. Please do,' she said quickly. Not that she was desperate for company or anything.

'I have been to Australia. New Zealand too.'

'Well, you're one up on me, then. I haven't seen New Zealand. In fact, I'd never been out of the country until I came here. Do you travel a lot?'

'Not now. I have commitments now that make travelling difficult. But when I was a young man, I wanted to see the world, and I travelled cheaply.'

'Ah. Backpacking?'

'Staying in hostels or with people I met. I suppose you would call it backpacking. I learned English as I went, because it was essential. I did some grape-picking and other temporary jobs.'

And she'd bet he was a huge hit with the girls. Although his English was perfect, he spoke it with an accent that was unmistakably French, and in his younger days he must have been incredibly attractive. It would have been a lethal combination.

He tilted his head. 'Are you here alone?'

'Yes.' For an instant Leonie wondered whether that was a smart admission, but then she dismissed the thought. Stranger or not, he didn't seem the least bit dangerous. And it wasn't as if he knew where she was staying. Sitting in this crowded café with Jean-Claude behind the counter, there was no risk at all.

As if he'd picked up on her hesitation, he said, 'I did not mean to intrude.'

'No, no, you're not intruding.' She hadn't meant to give that impression.

'I noticed that you preferred this newspaper last time.' He held out the rolled-up publication that he'd been holding. 'It is not as heavy-going as that one.' Gesturing at the one on the table, he got to his feet. 'Now, I will leave you to your reading.'

'Oh, okay.' Disappointed that their conversation was to be cut short, she said quickly, 'I'm Leonie, by the way. Perhaps I'll see you in here again?'

He smiled then, and Leonie felt the unfamiliar zing of…of appreciation, not attraction. It was just that she hadn't seen such a good-looking man for a very long time. If ever. And his smile should come with a warning. If she'd been someone else—someone younger, someone…well, whatever—it would have knocked her off her feet. But she was a wife and mother. Well, she *had been* a wife, and was still a mother. She was well past all that.

Besides, she was sitting down.

'I hope so. I come here often.'

But he was still a stranger, and had she really just suggested meeting him again when she knew nothing about him? What was she doing?

He held out his hand. 'My name is Jacques Broussard. I am an old friend of the owner here,' he said, nodding towards Jean-Claude. 'Our families have known each other for years. If you want to check up on me, that is.'

Leonie grimaced. 'Did you just read my mind?'

With a grin, he said, 'Mind-reading is not one of my talents. But you seem like a sensible woman, and any sensible woman should take care when talking to strangers.'

'Yes, well, I'm Leonie Winters. Pleased to meet you. And thank you for this.' She tapped the news-paper he'd given her. 'I was struggling with the other one.'

He nodded. 'That's understandable, and you're welcome.'

After he'd gone, Leonie sat for a long moment. *Jacques Broussard.* What a name. Very…um, French. She could still feel his grasp on her hand as if he'd left an imprint. Glancing at her hand, she shook her head, dismissing the idea as ridicu-lous.

The last time anyone had shaken her hand was at Shane's funeral. Before she could stop them, memories of that day flooded her mind, forcing out every other thought. Many of his former em-ployees had approached her to shake her hand, to pay their respects. Tears filled her throat as she relived the emotional outpouring of admiration from people who'd known her husband. Shane had inspired the high opinion of everybody who had had meaningful contact with him, mainly through his work ethic and his one-hundred-per-cent commitment to anything he undertook.

He'd been committed to her. How lucky was she?

Not only had she married her high-school sweetheart, but they'd remained in love throughout twenty years of marriage. Not many couples could say that nowadays.

They'd been blessed by the arrival of two wonderful children who'd never caused them the anguish that she'd witnessed other families undergoing. Theirs had been a close and happy family unit.

That was why she'd never had a holiday without her family, and they'd shared some amazing experiences, albeit close to home in case Shane should have been called back to work to deal with an emergency. He'd enjoyed spending time with his family, but had never lost sight of his responsibilities. He'd taken them seriously; he'd taken everything seriously, actually, even his health. So it was unfair that, despite all his care, he'd still fallen ill.

She'd tried to make him well, and when it had become clear that he wouldn't recover she'd done her best to make him happy, or, at the very least, comfortable. She'd tried hard, and he'd appreciated it. Never grumpy, never complaining, he'd thanked her every day for the sacrifices she was making.

Huh. As if she'd cared about what she was missing out on. Nothing had been as important as spending every moment with Shane, nursing him herself rather than hand over the chores to a paid carer.

What would Shane think of her now? She'd abandoned her children with the frivolous goal of learning another language. And what use would it be to her?

Once she left Nice for home, she'd probably never visit France again. Why should she, having got it out of her system?

What was she doing here? Just wasting time and money?

Or was she looking for something? Her own life?

The tears had gradually made their way from her throat to her eyes and one spilled over her lower lid onto the newspaper that Jacques had given her. She stared down at the absorbent paper as it made the teardrop look much worse than it was.

Which was exactly what *she* was doing.

She had to lighten up. It was three years since Shane had died and most of the time she was fine.

It was only on odd occasions that memories set her off. She was incredibly lucky to be in the position she was in. How many women had the opportunity to do exactly what they'd always wanted to do?

Wiping away the remaining tears before they could fall, she remembered something that Jacques had said.

He'd noticed which newspaper she preferred last week.

He'd been watching her, taking notes—not literally, she assumed, but still… She didn't know whether to be flattered or concerned.

Perhaps she should do as he'd suggested and check his references. But a glance at the smiling Jean-Claude had her shaking her head. That wasn't necessary. Just the fact that he'd suggested it was enough to tell her he had nothing to hide and, besides, what were they talking about here? A chat, that was all. Not a date.

So, he was observant. That wasn't a bad thing. He probably noticed stuff about everyone who entered the café. It wouldn't hurt *her* to be more aware of her surroundings. She'd been living in the very small world consisting of her immediate family for far too long.

CHAPTER TWO

THE next day, when Leonie arrived back at the apartment at the end of her lessons, she didn't wait for claustrophobia to hit, but immediately showered and changed her clothes before checking her reflection in the only mirror she had. A small one.

All the local women were well turned out, even when dressed in casual clothes. In comparison, she felt dowdy in her shorts and T-shirt. Sam had tried to convince her to shop for a whole new wardrobe before coming away, but she'd made do with popping to the local chain store and grabbing some basic items. She'd never been one for fashion. There had always been more important things to think about, family things, and no one had ever cared what she wore. As long as she was tidy, she'd figured fashion didn't matter.

She looked at herself more critically than she ever had before. Maybe she should visit some of the local shops and see what she could come up with? It couldn't hurt.

At least she was lucky that she hadn't gained much weight over the years, especially as she hadn't been skinny to start with. She'd always been a bit hippy and busty. Actually, she had gained quite a few kilos earlier on, but had lost them during the first months of Shane's illness. Seeing him suffer had turned her right off food, and she'd never really regained her former appetite. So, no, she wasn't fat, but that didn't mean her body was in great condition. Far from it.

Her hair was okay, though. Well, her hairdresser had offered to touch up a few grey roots, but she hadn't seen the point at the time, saying that they weren't noticeable amongst her blond hair and her natural curls hid them anyway.

She chewed her lip, wishing she'd let the hairdresser work her magic on those roots.

But why? Did she see the point now? Was Jacques the reason for her out-of-character critical scrutiny?

No!

She hoped to see Jacques again, true enough, but only because he was someone to talk to. Someone friendly. So what if she looked her age? He did too.

Hmm, like there was any comparison. Men

aged differently from women, and he looked great.

She sighed. If he was superficial enough to object to the way she looked, he wasn't someone she wanted as a friend. She couldn't help being over forty, and there was nothing wrong with that anyway.

Leonie pushed open the café door and was rewarded by the sight of Jacques, in another pristine white shirt, his dark suit jacket draped over the back of his chair. He rose to his feet and waved her over.

She sighed with relief. At least there would be no awkwardness such as deciding whether to go up to him or not.

'Good afternoon, Leonie.'

He pronounced her name 'Lay-o-nie', with the emphasis on the first syllable. She was about to correct him, when she changed her mind. It sounded different, and she liked it. Different was good.

'Hello, Jacques.'

Goodness, he was even more gorgeous than she'd remembered. Maybe this wasn't such a good idea?

But then he grinned, a grin so genuine and boyish it made her heart stand still. And she knew she couldn't walk away.

He placed a chair next to his and held it for her. She gave him a questioning look. Why would she sit next to him like that?

He shrugged. As if he'd read her mind again, he said, 'I thought we could read the newspaper at the same time. You can point out anything you have difficulty with and I can help you.'

'Oh, but you don't have to—' She stopped, because it was thoughtful of him. She smiled. 'Thank you. That's a nice idea. I appreciate it.'

After she'd settled at the table and Jacques had fetched her a coffee, Leonie took her reading glasses from her bag and slipped them on. Then she watched Jacques reach into his jacket pocket and do the same thing.

Grinning, she said, 'It's a drag, isn't it? A sign of old age creeping up on us.'

'We have a lot of life in us yet.'

'Oh, I don't know about that.' She shrugged. 'Maybe you do, but my best years are well and truly gone.'

He frowned. 'Why do you say that?'

'It's a fact. I've been married, had my children, now I've turned forty and I'm heading towards…' With a pang, she realised she didn't know what she was heading towards. 'Well, grandchildren, I guess.'

He made a scoffing sound. 'You are not old enough to be a grandmother.'

'Well, technically I am, but, more to the point, I wouldn't like either of my kids to have children yet. I hope they'll get an education and live a little before they settle down to raising a family.'

She sighed, looking away.

'You miss them?'

'I do. I miss them so much. Yesterday, I was seriously considering going home. This...' she waved a hand meant to encompass the café, the city, the course...everything '...this is *so* not me. I'm a mother first and foremost, and I can hardly believe I've left my children to fend for themselves while I'm here, pleasing myself.'

She shrugged, then took her phone from her bag, flipped it open and brought a photo of Sam to the screen. 'This is my daughter, Samantha. She's the elder of the two.'

He smiled. 'She is very pretty. She takes after her mother.'

Leonie's eyes widened, just for an instant, but then she reminded herself that it was the sort of thing people said to be polite. He was right about one thing, though. Sam *was* very pretty. But she was sweet too.

With a proud smile, she nodded. 'She's a lovely girl. She's studying social work at university. It's always been her ambition to help people.'

'You must have raised her well.'

'Oh, no. It's all her own doing. Even as a toddler she was like that. At kindergarten she used to get terribly upset if one of the other children fell and scraped a knee. Empathy. That's her strongest trait.'

It felt so good to talk about her kids. Her fellow students were barely older than Sam and Kyle and had no interest whatsoever in her maternal ramblings. But Jacques didn't seem bored.

He gave her an encouraging nod as she brought up a picture of Kyle. She turned the phone to face him.

'He does not look so much like you.'

'He looks just like his father did at the same age.'

Shane had been just the opposite of Jacques. Taller, and lanky. His limbs had seemed too long for him at school and he'd never really grown into them. Blond, with a serious face. It was the seriousness that had attracted her to him in the first place. He was different from the other boys at school.

Jacques gave her a curious look. 'You said you had been married? You are no longer…?'

'I was married to Shane for twenty years. Till he died. Three years ago.'

'I'm sorry.'

She nodded. 'He'd been ill for a long time.' She took a sip of coffee.

After a pause, he said, 'Three years is not such a long time. You must miss him still.'

'Oh, I do.' Yes, she missed Shane, and she always would, but she no longer woke during the night shocked to find he wasn't there. She hadn't done that for months now. She'd even taken her wedding ring off, and tucked it away safely in her jewellery box at home. She was getting used to being alone. 'I do miss having him there to talk to about the kids, and to make plans with. Though, to be honest, we hadn't really made any plans for a long time.'

She stopped for another sip of coffee.

'Tell me about your son,' Jacques said.

This brought a smile to her face again as she looked up, and she guessed that had been his intention.

'He's great too, but in a very different way from Samantha. He's such a boy.' Then, not sure that Jacques would understand what she meant, she went on. 'He loves action movies and football and off-road driving with his mates. He drives Sam to distraction. When they were kids he used to torment her with creepy crawlies and the like, but he thinks the world of his sister and wouldn't let anyone hurt her.'

Physically, at least, she thought. There was nothing Kyle or she could do to stop Sam being hurt by people who took advantage of her soft heart, as they'd discovered already.

Sighing, she lifted her head to look into Jacques' brown eyes. 'And what about you? Married? Children?'

He hesitated, then reached into his pocket and pulled out a wallet. After opening it, he gazed at it for a moment before turning it so that Leonie could see two photos. 'My son. Antoine.'

She leaned forward to get a better look, and saw a boy who obviously had Jacques' genes. 'Oh, gosh, he looks just like you.'

And being in his father's arms made it that much more obvious. But as she had the thought she also registered that he was kind of big to be carried by his father.

Shifting her eyes to the second picture, she saw the reason. In this one, Antoine was on his own, and in a wheelchair.

She looked up. 'He's cute. How old is he?'

'Ten. These photos were taken a year ago.'

She nodded. 'And the wheelchair?' She could have ignored it, but that wasn't in her nature. Her question was straightforward because she wanted to know the answer.

'Spina bifida. He has no feeling in his legs.'

'I see.'

'And to answer your other question…' Jacques paused, and put his wallet away before continuing '…I *was* married. Antoine's mother left while he was still very young. We were divorced twelve months later.'

Leonie's jaw dropped and for a moment she stared at him. 'She left?'

He nodded. 'She couldn't cope.'

'Couldn't *cope*? But surely you could have got help?'

'Yes, yes.' He waved a hand. 'It wasn't the work involved, it was…' He paused and cleared his throat. 'She was a perfectionist. Everything in her life had to be one-hundred-per-cent perfect. In her eyes, Antoine was…defective.'

'Defective?' She spluttered the word, then pursed her lips for a moment. 'Oh, my, I think it was better that she did leave if that was her attitude.'

'Exactly.'

Leonie blew out a breath. 'So, is it just you and him now?'

'We live with my mother and my brother. It wouldn't be practical for the two of us to live alone. Some aspects of Antoine's care require more than one pair of hands, especially now that he is growing older and heavier. I couldn't manage him on my own, and, besides, I have to work.'

'Yes, of course.'

'At the risk of sounding…what is the word? Soppy. He is the most important thing in my life.'

'It's not soppy. I mean, yes, that's the right word, but I understand completely. Like I said, I came very close to going home because I miss my two so much.'

'What stopped you?'

Would he be shocked to hear that *he* had? Probably, but it was true. Not because she had any silly ideas about him, just because it had done her heaps of good to make a connection, however small, with another human being. It was such a relief to know that she didn't have to spend her entire stay feeling lonely.

'I didn't want to give up on the course.' That was true too. 'I might not be very good at it, but I do want to improve. It's supposed to be a really good course. It uses all the latest audio-visual methods, and language labs and so on, but I just feel left behind.'

He made a sympathetic sound.

'Maybe it's an age-related thing. If I was younger, I might be more receptive to it. I studied French at high school and I did quite well there, so I thought I'd be able to pick it up quickly. But that was a long time ago, and I was wrong.'

She sighed. 'I wish I could speak it as well as you speak English.'

'I'm sure you will, but it takes real-life

practice.' He drank some coffee and watched her over the rim of his cup. 'Anything worth doing takes practice. Lots of it.'

Now, what had made her read a double meaning into his perfectly innocent words?

The fact that he'd maintained eye contact a little longer than necessary?

She dismissed the nonsensical thought, quite sure he hadn't meant anything beyond what he'd said. And he was right. 'I shouldn't be speaking English now, should I? I should make an effort to talk to you in your own language. That's the only way to get practice, isn't it?

'The thing is, whenever I try to speak to anyone here in French, they smile indulgently and proceed to speak in English. It's…humbling. I'm obviously very bad at it.'

'Don't think of it as humbling, think of it as a compliment.'

She gave him a sceptical look.

'No, really. They are pleased that you have made the attempt, so they are returning the compliment by saving you the trouble.'

'Oh.' She laughed. 'I'll never get any practice, then, will I?'

'You can practise on me.'

She tilted her head. 'Really?'

'Really.'

'Are you sure I'm not keeping you from anything?'

'Not at all. I would have been here anyway.'

'But you would have been reading your newspaper and I'm stopping you from doing that.' She flapped a hand at it. 'I'm sorry.'

'Don't apologise. I have enjoyed hearing about your family.'

'Really?'

His lips twitched. '*Really.*' He waved a hand to bring her attention to the newspaper in front of them. '*Eh bien*, let's begin. Look, there is an interesting story here on page two.' He pointed it out. 'What do you think of that? Tell me in French, if you will.'

She smiled before bending her head. 'Sure, but it will take me a while to read it.'

'I can wait.'

They read in silence for some time, then discussed the story. With Jacques' encouragement and lots of laughter, Leonie stopped feeling embarrassed about her mistakes—and there were plenty of them—and started to enjoy herself, certainly a lot more than she'd enjoyed the lessons at the school.

They went on to discuss more stories, partly in one language, partly the other. An hour had gone by when Jacques announced that he had to leave.

Disappointed but determined not to show it, Leonie asked brightly, 'Back to work?'

He nodded as he rose to his feet.

'Do you mind if I ask where you work?'

Smiling, he said, 'Do you know the restaurant La Bergamote?'

'No, I'm afraid not. Are you the chef?'

He shook his head. 'The owner.'

'Oh. But if you own a restaurant, why do you come here for coffee? That's a coals-to-Newcastle thing, isn't it?'

'A what?'

She shook her head. 'Figure of speech. It just seems a strange thing to do.'

'It's a tradition. I enjoy the walk and I like to see my friend.' He glanced towards Jean-Claude. 'Also, it's good to get away from tourists, just for an hour or so between lunch and dinner.'

'And today you've had to put up with me,' she said with a rueful grimace. 'I won't bother you again. I'll let you enjoy your coffee in peace in future.' She meant what she said, but she was already imagining how lonely she'd be without their conversation to look forward to.

'No.' He frowned. 'Please don't. I will look forward to seeing you here again.'

Was he just saying that to humour her? She gave him a direct look and he returned her gaze steadily. Either he was telling the truth or he had a very good poker face.

'Tomorrow afternoon, yes?'

'I guess so.'

'I will be devastated if you are not here.'

'Devastated.' She laughed. 'Yeah, right.' But she appreciated his kindness. 'I'll see you tomorrow, then.'

He smiled. 'Good.' With a nod at her and a wave for his friend behind the counter, he swung his jacket over his shoulder. She couldn't help noticing that he was quite solid, masculine. Not big, but even through his white shirt she could tell that he was well defined, strong-looking.

By the time he'd left, Leonie was feeling happier and more relaxed than she had since she'd arrived in France.

Jacques walked away, wondering whether he'd gone mad. He usually had to know people quite well before he told them about Antoine. He certainly never discussed his ex-wife. So, why had he opened up to Leonie that way?

Leonie had been surprisingly easy to talk to. His intention at the start of the conversation had been to make her feel comfortable so that she would relax and talk to him, but she had been the one who'd made him talk.

Well, in fact, they had both talked, and he now knew about her husband. He wasn't sure whether she was over him yet. And he'd learned about her children. He hadn't been lying when he'd told her he enjoyed hearing about them, but it was what her words told him about *her* that he'd enjoyed most. Her pride in them had been tangible, and pleasing.

He was going to take pleasure in helping Leonie to learn his language.

On Saturday, Jacques strode towards the café. He'd met Leonie each afternoon for the past three days, but today he was late. He lengthened his stride a little more. He did not want to miss her.

Just as he'd had the thought the café came into view and he saw Leonie walking away from it, in the opposite direction.

He called out to her, breaking into a jog. When she looked back and saw him, she didn't appear angry or irritated as he'd worried she might. Instead, she gave him a broad smile.

'I'm sorry,' he said when he reached her, more pleased to see her than he had any right to be. 'I couldn't get here sooner.'

He stopped to draw breath and Leonie touched his forearm in concern. 'What happened? Is everything all right now?'

Her sincere expression touched him too, but inside, throwing him off balance.

'Yes. Yes, it is,' he said, recovering his equilibrium. 'Did you get my message?'

She nodded. 'Jean-Claude told me you'd been held up. That was thoughtful of you, to call the café. When it got so late, I decided you weren't coming at all today.'

'I wasn't sure I'd get here in time. Where are you going? Back to your apartment?'

'No. I'm staying over there.' She gestured vaguely. 'Not far from Place Garibaldi, in Rue Saint Augustin.'

It struck him that they'd come a long way in a few days. At the beginning, she wouldn't have told him where she lived, which was good—he didn't like to think of her being vulnerable to unscrupulous people who might take advantage of her kindness. She didn't deserve to be ripped off. But today, she hadn't hesitated to reveal her address…as if she trusted him.

The thought gave him a jolt.

'I was just going for a walk,' she said. 'Nowhere in particular.'

'May I join you?'

'Yes, of course, but are you certain you wouldn't rather go back?' She pointed to the café. 'Don't you want a coffee?'

He shook his head and turned in the direction she'd been walking, adjusting his steps to match her shorter ones as they set off.

'It was one of my kitchen staff,' he said. 'She has been having problems with her husband and she made the decision to leave him.'

'Oh?'

For the first time, a look of disapproval crossed her face. Perhaps she found it hard to accept that not all marriages were as long and happy as hers had been. But it was a sad fact of life that some marriages were not made in heaven. His own included.

He shook off the bad memory before it could spoil this pleasant moment with Leonie.

'He was violent,' he said. 'She made the right choice.'

'Oh, I see. Of course she did. That's awful.' Her forehead creased. 'But how were you involved?'

He shrugged. 'She needed someone to help move her belongings out of the house while her husband was at work. She needed to find a safe place for her children and herself to stay where he is unlikely to find them.'

'She has children?' Biting her lip, she frowned. 'Did she find somewhere to stay?'

'Yes. She's safe now.'

'Oh, good.' She blew out a breath. 'You helped her do all this?'

He nodded. 'Someone had to. It took a little longer than I expected.'

'For what it's worth, I think you did absolutely the right thing.' After a hesitation, she said, 'Is she your girlfriend?'

'No! Of course not. I told you, she is married.'

'I don't think that would stop everyone.'

'It would stop me.'

She gave him a doubtful glance.

'You don't believe me?'

'Of course I do. But I don't understand why you felt obliged to help.'

He shrugged. 'She has no one else.'

Smiling, she shook her head. 'You're a nice man, Jacques.'

'Let's go this way.' He touched her elbow with one hand as he pointed with the other. Embarrassed, he drew her attention to the baroque architecture of the church in front of them.

He watched her as she looked up at the building. She might be over forty, but she was quite beautiful, and not at all aware of the fact.

He'd noticed her as soon as she'd entered Jean-Claude's café that first day with the light from the door shining through her blond curls and making a striking picture. Then she'd turned her gaze on him and it was so direct, so frank, that he'd been taken aback for a second or two.

Hers wasn't the classical beauty he'd always preferred, but she had a charming, expressive face, a genuine smile and eyes as blue as the Mediterranean, eyes that warmed at the slightest mention of her children.

She seemed surprised to find herself here playing truant from her role as a mother. Leonie, it seemed, had never taken time for herself and was long overdue for a break. As they moved on she stared up at the pastel-coloured façades of the buildings they were passing.

'Why did you choose to stay in Vieux Nice?'

'The old town? Well, I thought it would be full of character. And it is. These build-ings…they're so tall and thin and so close together. It's as if they're reaching up for the sun.'

Jacques chuckled. 'You have a point.'

'But they're so pretty too. I love all the shutters on the windows. They're like eyelids.'

'Eyelids?' He frowned, wondering whether he'd misunderstood the meaning of the English word, but then he realised what she meant. 'Eyelids. That's different.'

'It's colourful and cheerful.'

He nodded. 'It's a popular area now. At one time it was crime-infested and poverty-stricken, but it's changed. There has been a lot of restoration work to preserve its architecture, and urban regeneration has encouraged the young, trendy people to move in. In fact, the further east you go in Nice, the younger the population becomes.'

'Oh.' Leonie laughed. 'I didn't know that. Perhaps I should have chosen the other end of town.'

'I didn't say it for that reason. You are not old, Leonie. You have to stop talking of yourself that way.'

'Why? It doesn't bother me.'

It bothered him. She was a vibrant, beautiful woman, and her age was an irrelevant number. 'Besides, it's not all young people. There are some lifelong residents here too.'

'Yes, I've seen some older people. There's a lady who always sits at the window opposite mine.'

They continued walking through the labyrinth of streets packed with shops, galleries and bistros. Leonie stopped to look into a store selling handmade toys and puppets, then they made their way to the Quai des États-Unis where they stopped to gaze at the glimmering sea.

'That ferry is going to Corsica,' he said, pointing at a yellow ship.

She nodded, shading her eyes from the high afternoon sun as she followed its progress. 'Do you have to get back to the restaurant now?'

He frowned at his watch, wishing it would slow down. 'Soon. I have time to walk back with you, though.'

'Don't let me delay you.' She turned to him with a smile. 'I can find my own way back. Sort of. Well, I might take a detour or two, but I'll get there eventually.'

He watched her for a moment, the wind blowing her curls into a chaotic mess, then shook his head. 'I'd like to walk back with you, if you're ready to go.'

'Sure.' She gave him one of her beaming smiles.

'Have you visited the flower market?' he asked as they turned.

'No. I've heard about it, but apparently you have to be there early and I'm at the school every morning.'

'Sunday too?'

She shook her head. 'There are no classes on Sunday.'

'Then you should see it. The best time is around six o'clock while the tourists are still in their hotel rooms.'

'Six! All right, I'll set my alarm and make sure I do.'

'I could collect you, if you like.'

'Really? Would you?'

'Of course.' The idea of spending the morning with her appealed, and her happy smile warmed him.

'What a lovely idea. I'd really like that.'

He nodded. 'I would too.'

And he meant it. It had been a long time since he'd found a woman's company so enjoyable. It had been a long time since he'd known a woman like Leonie. If he ever had.

CHAPTER THREE

LEONIE was watching from her little balcony when Jacques turned into the Rue Saint Augustin just before six o'clock. With a smile at her early-rising neighbour across the street, who surprised her by smiling back, she closed the doors and hurried downstairs to meet him.

'*Bonjour*, Leonie.'

A little thrill ran through her at the way he said her name and she grinned at him. '*Bonjour*, Jacques.'

She slipped on her sunglasses, and felt a lot younger than her years as they made their way to the market, chatting about all sorts of things. There was an ease between them that was reassuring, but at the same time amazing. On the one hand, it felt as if she'd known him for ages, but, on the other, everything she learned about him was new and intriguing.

She learned that he liked art—a lot—and was

very proud of French artists whom she only knew by name, and vaguely at that.

'French people like to look at beautiful things,' he said.

'But that's a generalisation. I mean, you can't say that other nationalities *don't* like to look at beautiful things. How are the French different?'

His face twisted in thought. 'I don't know how to explain it, but we *are* different.'

She laughed. She could well believe it. 'I know nothing about art.'

'But you must know whether you like a painting, or not?'

'I suppose I would know, but I've never really looked at any.'

His horrified expression made her laugh again. It was going to be fun learning all the differences between them. Like turning to page one of a new book, so much to discover.

She couldn't remember the last time she'd been so excited about a new friend. At one point she caught herself practically skipping with childish enthusiasm, and shook her head, smiling.

'What?'

'Nothing. Just that I haven't been out so early before, and it feels good. I like it.'

And she liked not being alone, she added silently. She had to be careful not to take advantage of Jacques' good nature. It would be very tempting to hint at other sights she wanted to see. But putting him in that position wouldn't be fair.

When they reached the *cours*, the streetlamps were still on, but a pink glow above the buildings promised that the sun would soon be with them. Market awnings stretched in front of Leonie. Stripes everywhere. Yellow and white, blue and white, yellow and green.

Cut flowers perfumed the fresh morning air, but it was the beautifully presented fruit and vegetables, and the herbs and spices, that surprised Leonie.

'I thought it was only flowers.' She pointed at one of the stalls. 'Look at the way that fruit has been arranged. Now, that's like a work of art.'

They walked the entire length of the market, a hundred stalls or more, seeing everything from golfball-sized stuffed olives to live chickens.

Her stomach jumped when he touched her back to steer her out of the way of flailing elbows, and towards an item he wanted her to see.

Leonie tried to put her reaction out of her mind. She'd been taken by surprise, that was all. She took her time over choosing a mixed bunch of flowers to brighten her apartment. Dominated by yellow lilies and white daisies with touches of orange and purple, it made her smile as she joined Jacques, who was waiting without any sign of impatience.

'Isn't it gorgeous? It will look lovely on my little table.'

She strolled at his side, acutely aware of him despite the mingling scents, the noise and jostle of the market.

She wanted him to touch her again so she could see if she'd imagined the electricity that had zipped through her. But at the same time, she didn't want him to touch her because she hadn't reacted like this to a man in…well, in for ever, and it was scary.

She couldn't even remember feeling such a strong response to Shane in the early days. But maybe it was her memory that was the problem. It had been a very long time, after all, since she and Shane had gone from classmates to boyfriend and girlfriend.

Yes, a long, long time.

And Jacques would probably be horrified. He was being friendly to her because…well, just because he was a nice man. Not because he saw her as anything other than a middle-aged woman who was trying to learn his language.

She tried to jolt herself out of her disturbing awareness of him, because there was no way she was going to let Jacques see what his presence was doing to her.

When they'd finally seen enough, they stood

for a moment in front of the tall, washed-out yellow house where Jacques said the artist Henri Matisse had lived early in the previous century, then he pointed and said, 'What do you think about climbing *la colline du château*?'

'Hmm?' She turned around to see the hill that rose from the edge of the old town. 'There's a *château* up there?'

'No. There was, once, a long time ago. There's a waterfall, and a park.'

'I like waterfalls.'

'There are lots of steps. We can use the lift, if you prefer.'

'One minute you're telling me not to say I'm old, and the next you're implying that I'm elderly and infirm.'

'I did not.' He frowned. 'That was not what I meant.'

She laughed at his consternation. 'I'm only teasing. Come on, let's go. But we'll walk.'

As they weaved their way slowly up the side of the hill, Leonie took in the increasingly breathtaking views of Nice below. At the top, they made their way straight to the viewing platforms.

'Oh, my word,' Leonie gasped. It was the first time she'd seen the harbour, and the number of three-storey yachts, millionaires' toys, moored in the neat rectangular harbour stunned her. For the first time since her arrival it sank in that this was the Riviera, the playground of the rich and famous.

Turning a hundred and eighty degrees, she gazed across the red roofs of the old town to the city and the more distant mountains. After a long, spellbound moment, Leonie sighed. 'I'm glad we made the hike. It was worth it.'

She looked back at the harbour, then turned away. 'Even if there is no *château*, which is a pity because I would love to see a real French *château*.'

'Then you need to go for a drive,' Jacques said as they walked away from the platform and wandered through the park.

'I know.' She shrugged. 'Never mind.'

'What do you mean?'

Leonie had stopped to watch some children on the playground, their laughter carrying to her as they scrambled up a rope climbing frame. She looked over her shoulder. 'What do I mean?'

'I don't understand. Don't you want to visit anywhere else?'

'Oh, well, yes, of course I'd like to, but I'm not going to drive a car on the wrong side of the road, and I have no sense of direction, and besides...' She shook her head. 'I don't enjoy sightseeing on my own.' Rolling her eyes, she said, 'Now I sound pathetic.'

'No, you don't. I can understand that.' He hesitated, then said, 'I could take you.'

'What? No.' She flapped her hands at him. 'You're too busy. You can't do that.'

'I can. My staff can manage on their own for a day. I've left them before, occasionally, when I've needed to take Antoine to an appointment, for instance.'

'But that's different. I don't want to put you to so much trouble just for me.'

He nodded. 'I'd like to take you for a drive, but it's your choice.' He lifted his shoulders, his eyes glinting in the sun. 'If you don't want me to, I'll understand.'

'Well, of course it's not that I don't *want* you to…it's just… Are you sure?'

He shrugged. 'Of course. Why would I have said it if I wasn't sure?'

She tilted her head to the side as excitement bubbled inside her. 'Would you really take me to see a *château*?'

'Yes.'

'Then, I'd love to. It won't matter if I miss a day's lessons tomorrow.'

'Not tomorrow.' He grimaced. 'I should have said. Tomorrow I'll be with Antoine. I'm sorry, he's expecting me. I don't like to disappoint him.'

'Oh.' Leonie smiled brightly to hide the fact

that she was ridiculously disappointed. 'No, of course you don't. No problem.'

He put one hand on his hip and pushed the other through his hair. 'You're disappointed.'

'*No*. Goodness, I'm not a child. Whenever you can spare the time will be fine.'

She took a deep breath. She wasn't sure whether her disappointment came from having the trip postponed, or from the thought of not seeing Jacques for a couple of days. But, either way, she certainly didn't begrudge him the chance to spend a day with his son. Not at all.

They walked on through the park, saw a museum that had been built to resemble a Roman ruin, and the impressive waterfall, but best of all Leonie loved the stepping stones with intricate mosaics which Jacques told her depicted scenes from Homer's *Odyssey*.

'Sam and Kyle would have loved these when they were kids,' she said, stepping from one to another.

He smiled, sadly, she thought. Then she remembered that his son would never have been able to use them as stepping stones. Her heart hammered and her stomach rolled at her insensitivity. She made a mental note to think before she spoke in future, because the last thing she wanted was to be hurtful to Jacques.

Half of the morning had gone by when they

stopped at a lawned area where Leonie sat on the ground, put her flowers down beside her and stretched out her legs. She wasn't used to so much exercise. 'Cripes, I feel unfit.'

She watched Jacques as he sat down near her. He had such a smooth, fluid way of moving, nothing awkward or clumsy about him. She enjoyed herself for a moment, just watching him, then looked away, embarrassed that she'd been staring.

Out of the corner of her eye she saw Jacques check his watch, and guessed he'd soon have to be making tracks.

'Come to La Bergamote for lunch,' he said suddenly.

She blinked. 'Are you serious?'

'Do you have other plans?'

'No.'

'It's Sunday. You shouldn't eat Sunday lunch alone.'

Sunday had always been a family day. Shane had loved his Sunday roast, and the kids had always made sure they were home for this one, even if they didn't make it for all the other meals she cooked during the week. She wondered if Sam and Kyle would eat together while she was away. She hoped so.

No, she didn't want to eat alone, and it would be very interesting to see Jacques' restaurant, she thought as she moistened her wind-dried lips. 'Thank you. I'd like that.'

'Good.' He smiled and her stomach twisted itself into a knot.

'I need to put these in water, though,' she said, gesturing at the flowers. And she needed to change her clothes, she thought, looking down at her navy shorts and T-shirt. The white denim jacket she'd worn over the top, since it had been chilly at six in the morning, was now on the ground beside her. She didn't know how classy Jacques' restaurant would be, but she would bet on it requiring something dressier than this outfit.

'No problem. I can wait for you.'

La Bergamote was intimate and crowded and buzzing with conversation. Leonie enjoyed watching the smart clientele who were clearly there for both the good food and the sense of being somewhere special.

What she didn't enjoy so much was feeling unstylish and out of her league. She'd changed into a tiered cotton skirt with a plain white, close-fitting T-shirt, which was about as dressy as she could manage. She made a decision right then that she would spend Monday afternoon shopping for clothes. The next time she came to eat at La Bergamote, she intended to fit right in. If there was a next time, of course. This could turn out to be a one-off invitation, but she hoped not, it was such a great place.

Located just off the Promenade des Anglais, which ran the length of the seafront, the restaurant was a long, narrow room, lit by old-fashioned sconce lamps even though it was the middle of the day, with plum-coloured banquettes along the walls and dark wood tables and chairs. It was elegant and refined, but also gave the impression of solidity. Much like Jacques, she thought with a smile.

She watched as he moved about the restaurant, looking absolutely fantastic in his dark suit, which he must have changed into in one of the back rooms. She sighed. Suit, jeans, it didn't seem to matter…

She might as well admit it to herself. She was attracted to Jacques in a way she'd never been attracted to a man. Ever. All this heat and tingling and electricity business was new to her. But she had no intention of getting involved with another man. She'd been married to Shane for twenty years. He was the love of her life. Even if he was no longer here, she had her memories, and they would be enough to keep her warm for the rest of her life.

Still, it was a revelation to meet someone like Jacques and discover that, even now, she possessed hormones. That was where these feelings came from. Hormones doing their stuff to her nerve endings. She knew that much, but she'd thought they were a thing of her past; it was many years since she'd felt them stir, and even then...

Well, she could and would ignore them because hormones weren't real, or, at least, their effects were only transitory. What she'd had with Shane was real. They'd had a family. And that family was waiting for her back in Australia.

This new friendship with Jacques was important to her, and she wanted it to continue because it was making her time here in Nice so much more enjoyable. A visit to the flower market would have been interesting on her own, but not nearly as interesting as it had been with Jacques. And he'd promised to take her to see a *château*, which was a treat she hadn't expected to experience.

So, yes, she wanted to continue to be friends with Jacques, but from now on she was going to ignore her attraction to him. Friendship was going to be the only thing on her mind. She wouldn't allow those silly hormones to dictate how she felt about being in his company.

'I'm sorry to keep you waiting, Leonie,' Jacques said when he finally approached the small table.

'No problem. I can see that you're busy.' She hesitated, head tilted, while he sat down, then said, 'What do you actually do? I mean, I know you're the owner, but there's a chef and a maître d'…'

He laughed. 'You make me sound superfluous.'

'No, no…' She shook her head. 'I'm interested, that's all.'

He gave a small shrug. 'A restaurant is a business. It needs managing. Someone has to worry about recruiting the right people to maintain a standard, about keeping the dining room full, about paying the bills.'

'Of course. I never thought about it. I've never known anyone who owned a restaurant before.'

'Also, I like to meet the customers. We have regulars—some have been coming here for many years. It is only polite to greet them personally and assure them that they are welcome, don't you think?'

'Oh, absolutely, but you said many years… How long have you owned the restaurant?'

'It has been in the Broussard family for a long time. My grandfather started it, and he left it to me when he died. It's one of the most popular restaurants in the region.'

'Oh, how wonderful. You must be very proud of it.'

He smiled and gave a single nod. 'I am. And now, what are you going to eat?'

She slipped on her reading glasses. She'd

already looked at the menu, which was in both French and English, but she still didn't know what to choose. 'It all sounds so lovely. I was hoping you might recommend something.'

He pointed out a few recommendations, then leaned back and made a subtle sign to the head waiter, who hurried over to them.

Leonie smiled at the immaculately dressed waiter and carefully pronounced her selections in French.

Jacques nodded his encouragement. 'Would you like me to order the wine?'

'Yes, please.'

Jacques spoke rapidly to his employee, who inclined his head in agreement before collecting the menus and hurrying off.

'So,' Leonie said, 'why hasn't a nice man like you been snapped up?'

He turned a puzzled gaze on her. 'Snapped up?'

'Why haven't you remarried?'

'Ah.'

He said no more and his silence made her stomach tighten. 'Or have you?'

Not that she should care. Hadn't she just told herself there was nothing between them but friendship?

'No. No, I have not.' He lifted his eyes to meet hers. 'But I came close. It was a bad time, and I haven't told anyone else about this.'

She could believe it. In her experience, men didn't talk about personal stuff, especially where pain was involved. She sat up a little straighter, conscious of an intense curiosity. 'How long ago?'

His eyes flickered away, then returned to her face. 'Around four years ago.'

Ridiculous to think he wouldn't have been tempted to marry again. And, of course, he would have had plenty of opportunity, a man as good-looking as him, a man who, as far as she could see, had everything going for him.

He looked down at his place setting and moved his cutlery a millimetre or so. 'It didn't work out.'

'Can I ask why?'

He met her eyes. 'Antoine.'

With a little shake of her head, she frowned. 'He didn't like her?'

He gave her a crooked smile. 'On the contrary, he adored her.' He shrugged. 'What can I say? My son has inherited my poor taste.'

'Then…?'

'She, it turned out, saw me as…' he looked up, frowning, and seemed to be searching for words '…a meal ticket is the expression, if I remember correctly.'

Leonie nodded, then bit her lip as she waited for him to go on.

'When I explained to her that I would want Antoine to move in with us after our marriage, and live here in Nice, just the three of us, she decided I wasn't such a good bargain. I think she'd expected that he would stay with his grandmother while we lived the life of a childless couple here in Nice.'

'Oh, Jacques.' She couldn't help herself; she reached for his hand where it lay on the table.

'For me, I suppose I was lucky to find out what she was like before it became too late, but for Antoine it was heartbreaking.'

Her heart ached for both him and his son. 'But surely he didn't know the reason—'

'No, no,' he said quickly, his expression horrified. 'But even so, he took her rejection personally. He was already attached to her, and believed she would be his stepmother.'

Leonie pursed her lips. 'Poor darling.'

'I can't let that happen again. He is a very sensitive boy.'

After lifting his empty wine glass and examining it, he said, 'Well, there's no chance of it happening again anyway. I'm too old to think about marriage now. I've been single for too long. Any relationships I have will be…casual.' He shrugged. 'No need for Antoine to know about them.'

The glass made a small thud on the tablecloth as

he put it down. Like a full stop for the conversation. And with perfect timing, the wine waiter arrived.

After tasting the sauvignon blanc, Jacques nodded his approval and both glasses were filled.

Leonie took a sip from hers and smiled. 'It's lovely. Good choice.'

Jacques smiled back. 'I thought you would like it.'

Casual relationships were a mystery to her; she didn't understand why anyone would embark on one. But then, she'd been lucky.

Jacques had his reasons, the main one being his belief that he was doing the right thing for his son, but she wasn't sure it was the right thing for him. It did seem sad that he'd never know the contentment of marriage. His first marriage didn't count. She shouldn't judge his ex-wife without knowing her, but it was hard not to assume that she was a horrible person. What kind of mother would leave her child like that, and for such a reason?

Her entrée turned up then. The endive in the *tarte tatin* had been caramelised until it was as sweet as an apple, but there was a lingering sharpness that contrasted with some creamy goat's cheese.

She wasn't a bad cook herself. She recalled the repertoire of nutritious meals she'd prepared from scratch, never failing to have a hot plate of food ready for the table when the family came home.

But when Shane had become sick, cooking had slipped down her list of priorities, especially as Sam and Kyle were happy to grab something while they were out, and she'd made do with a sandwich. She'd started cooking in earnest again over the last year or so. The kids might be fully grown, but they still needed a good, homemade meal to help them do their best in their studies, and she'd been determined to make up for any lack of maternal care while she'd been distracted looking after Shane.

She knew how to serve up a nice meal, but this was something else entirely. She finally understood why French food had such a glorious reputation. This was her first venture into a proper restaurant in France, and she was thrilled with it. And she was only on the first course.

Then there was the company. She slid a glance at Jacques. Something about his hands as he spread pâté on a slice of toasted brioche made her shiver inside.

Enough of that, she told herself. She'd decided to ignore these feelings, hadn't she?

He looked up just as she glanced across at him again.

'How is your food?' he asked.

'Beautiful. But you knew that, didn't you?' She smiled. 'Thanks for asking me here.'

'You're welcome.'

His eyes lingered on hers and she felt another shiver. Did she have no control over her hormones?

'You said you studied French in high school... Why did you wait so long to continue it?'

'Oh, you know.' She shrugged. 'I married Shane as soon as we left school and making a home got in the way of anything else I'd thought of doing.'

'What did your parents say about you marrying so young?'

She shrugged again. 'We were both the only child of a single parent. I think that was one of the reasons we were drawn to each other in the first place—we knew what each other was going through. Anyway, in my case, Dad just seemed relieved. I don't think he'd ever felt comfortable with the responsibility of raising a daughter alone. Mum died when I was born.'

She took a drink of wine and waited while their entrée plates were removed.

'Dad moved to Sydney and spent all his time drinking, from what I could tell. He'd always liked a beer, but it was as if he was free suddenly and making the most of it. Then, one night he staggered into the road where he was knocked down by a car and killed.'

'That's terrible. I'm sorry.'

Waving away his frown, she said, 'Yes, but by then I was pregnant with Sam, so I had something to take the edge off the shock, something to look forward to.'

She took a moment to gaze at the tiny fillets of sea bass sitting on a nest of delicate leaves, drizzled with a lemon dressing and accompanied by a stuffed squash flower. It looked too pretty to eat.

'And Shane's parent?'

She looked up. It was odd hearing someone else use Shane's name. Normally, people waited for her to bring him up, afraid that she'd collapse in tears at the mere mention of him. There was a time when that would have happened, so maybe those people were right to be wary. But now, she could hear his name spoken without becoming a blubbering mess.

'Shane's mum was disgusted.' She gave a rueful smile. 'I wasn't good enough for her son.'

'I can't believe it.' Jacques shook his head. *'Impossible.'*

She laughed at his indignant expression. 'Marriage wasn't what she wanted for her son at that age. And I can tell you, if Kyle had decided to marry at seventeen, I wouldn't have been happy either.'

'But it worked out for you both? You had a good marriage?'

'Oh, heck, yes. But I can't deny that it was hard

at the beginning. Shane was doing his plumbing apprenticeship so I had to work to bring in some money. I'd always wanted to be a nurse, but we couldn't afford for me to go to university.' She smiled. 'But I did enjoy my job in a primary school as a teacher's assistant. I loved working with the children.'

'Did you study later?'

'No, because we had our own children early, and I was helping Shane set up his business, so between those two jobs there was no time.'

And later, well, she'd had other priorities.

'What else did you want to do that you never managed to do?'

'Oh, there were all sorts of things I dreamed of doing, but I don't regret them in the same way.' She thought about it for a moment, then rolled her eyes. 'The usual things that girls dream about, I suppose. And, of course, I wanted to see the world. I do feel kind of embarrassed that this is my first time out of the country.'

'But you'll make up for that now? There will be other trips?'

'Mmm, maybe.'

His eyes narrowed. 'Don't say we have put you off?'

'Oh, no. It's just… I'm homesick, you know? You've been great and now I feel better about staying till the end of the course, but I miss the kids. And they need me there. They shouldn't have to concern themselves with the mundane chores of running a home when they have better things to do with their time.'

'Ah, but, if you do everything for them, they will never learn to look after themselves.'

'I know, but there's plenty of time for them to learn when they have to. And there will be time for me to travel then, if I still want to.'

He shook his head, not in an unkind way, but her wanting to be there for her kids didn't make her unique, it just made her a parent. 'I'm sure you'd be just the same if it was you and Antoine we were talking about.'

He laughed, rolling his eyes. 'You're right.'

A flash of colour caught her eye and she looked to her side in time to see a striking man in a yellow shirt walk up to the table. Jacques stood and greeted him in a way that told her this was an old friend before he introduced him as such. François had something to do with the film industry; she couldn't catch quite what it was because Jacques was talking in French and it was all she could do to keep up.

When he suggested joining the two of them at their table, it would have taken extraordinary rudeness on Jacques' part to refuse, so she forced down her irritation and smiled as if it were a great idea.

Soon, though, she forgot about being irritated and began to enjoy herself. François couldn't speak English and, as she didn't want to keep bothering Jacques to interpret, she had to concentrate. And François insisted on including her in the conversation as if she could understand every word.

She discovered that he was in movie production, and he told her some interesting stories about well-known actors who'd come to the South of France. He asked her masses of questions about Australia, appearing really interested in her answers. By dessert—*une île flottante*, an island of meringue floating in a lake of vanilla custard and topped by a swirl of spun sugar—she felt she'd learned a great deal more of the language than she had during her classes.

Jacques gritted his teeth and smiled. François was stretching their friendship to breaking point and if he didn't call an end to this meal soon, he might do something he'd regret.

François' good looks had always enabled him to get exactly what he wanted, and Jacques had, in the past, found it amusing to watch him work his charm, especially on susceptible women. Like

Leonie. There was nothing amusing about the scene in front of him, though.

She seemed to be spellbound by François' words, but Jacques was only half listening. There was nothing he hadn't heard before and he'd had enough of the way François leaned towards Leonie with that intent look on his face, because Jacques knew it was just an act. He did not want to see her laughing at any more of those well-used anecdotes. And he did not want to see her hurt by François.

When his so-called friend announced that he would escort Leonie back to her apartment as if no one else had a say in the matter, Jacques bit out, 'There is no need.'

He knew exactly what would happen when they got there, and he was having none of it.

'I am going to walk with her,' he told François.

'Oh, but I've taken up so much of your time already today.' Leonie smiled across the table. 'I'm sure you're both very busy, and I can find the way by myself.'

He shot a warning glance at his friend. 'I am not too busy, and I will walk with you.'

François put on a display of being heartbroken, and Leonie was still laughing when they left the restaurant and made their way onto the Promenade des Anglais. She looked beautiful with her blue eyes twinkling and the ocean breeze lifting the curls from her shoulders.

'He's good fun, isn't he?'

'Hmmph.'

She sent him a curious glance. 'What's the matter? Don't you like him? I thought he was a friend of yours.'

'He was, until today.'

'Oh.' She turned away, but he caught sight of her puzzled expression as she did so, and hated himself for spoiling her mood. If anyone needed to laugh and forget the troubles of her past, it was Leonie.

People strolled by in both directions and he sighed silently as he pushed his hands into his pockets.

'François is a…womaniser.'

Her head snapped around. 'Is he?'

He sighed again, aloud this time. 'I am only telling you this because you should be wary of him.'

'Me? Why me?'

'He was flirting with you.'

She let out a sudden snort of laughter. 'Flirting? With me?' Shaking her head, she said, 'Jacques, you were there. He wasn't doing any such thing.'

'He was,' he insisted.

Her laughter turned into a frown. 'He was only talking to me. We were having a conversation. All three of us.'

'Leonie, I know François well. I have known him for a very long time. I am telling you the truth when I tell you this. He wanted to walk back with you because he was hoping he could talk his way into your bed.'

Her eyebrows shot up and her cheeks flushed bright pink. It was a very attractive look, one that made him want to reach for her and hold her in his arms, but he kept his hands to himself. With difficulty.

'That's not funny. Why would you say that? There's no way it's true. François is very good-looking. Why on earth would he be interested in an old has-been like me?'

Shocked, he grasped her forearm and turned her to face him. 'Leonie, don't say that! You are an attractive woman. A *very* attractive woman. Any man would…'

His arms went around her, pulling her closer, and his gaze dipped to her pink lips, lingering there. Without thinking, he leaned towards them…but then he became conscious of her hands on his chest, pushing. He shook his head to clear it of the thought that had gripped him. The thought of kissing her.

'I'm sorry.' He dropped his hands. 'I did not mean to…'

She stared. 'You…you find me attractive?'

'Of course.'

'Of *course*?'

'You are a lovely, vivacious woman.' He shrugged. 'I would not be human if I did not.'

She closed her mouth and he saw her swallow before she said, 'I thought we were friends.'

'We are.'

'Just friends, I mean.'

He hesitated. 'If that's what you want.'

'I'm a widow, Jacques.' She swallowed again. 'You know that.'

He nodded. 'I know.'

'I…I've nev—' She stuttered a few more syllables, then looked confused.

'I'm sorry. I didn't mean to upset you.'

'I just… I think you might have the wrong idea about me.'

'No.'

He lifted a hand, intending only to touch her shoulder in a reassuring gesture, but she turned away, saying, 'I think I'll walk back on my own.'

'Leonie…wait.'

She shook her head, and set off rapidly along the seafront walk.

He watched her go, wondering whether he should go after her. He didn't want her to feel he was pestering her. That was the last thing he wanted.

He removed his suit jacket and, hooking a

finger into the collar, slung it over his shoulder as he turned to walk back to the restaurant. He was an idiot. He'd made a mess of what should have been a very pleasant walk. He'd spoiled a day that had been one of his most enjoyable in a long time, except for the anger over François.

There had been no need to warn her about François; she wasn't foolish enough to be talked into something she didn't want to do, but still he'd allowed François' intentions to get under his skin and frustrate him into a stupid move.

But, no, it wasn't François' fault. He hadn't known until the moment he'd come close to kissing her quite how much he wanted to kiss her. His skin burned at the memory. He couldn't blame anyone but himself.

He wasn't used to women running away from him. There hadn't been many of the casual relationships he'd mentioned to Leonie, but on those few occasions he'd dated there had never been any reticence on the part of the women. He'd been the one to hold back, not wanting to give them false hopes.

But this was different. He and Leonie weren't dating; they were friends, and until today he'd had no intention of trying to change that. But subconsciously he must have been hoping for an opportunity. Expelling a loud sigh, he told himself that he'd be lucky if she'd even talk to him again.

CHAPTER FOUR

LEONIE awoke in a sweat, the oversized T-shirt that she wore in bed twisted around her waist. For a stunned moment she lay there, wide-eyed.

She'd had a dream about a man other than her husband. Like no dream she'd ever had before. Guilt hit her in the stomach. She should *not* be lying there remembering…replaying the way Jacques' hands had felt on her skin, a memory that was so vivid, it was as if it had really happened.

Goodness knew how her imagination had conjured up some of the things that had occurred in that dream, because she'd never done any of them with Shane. The closest she'd come to such passion was reading about it in books.

Making love with Shane had been sweet and familiar, the coming together of two people who knew each other's bodies as well as they knew their own. There had been no…well, no passion.

And she had never missed it. You couldn't miss something you'd never had.

She got out of bed, pulled the T-shirt's hem down to mid-thigh, then walked over to the little kitchen where she poured herself a glass of water from the bottle in the fridge.

Shaking off the effects of the dream, or attempting to anyway, she recalled the moment after lunch when Jacques had almost kissed her.

It had only been a short time before—just before lunch, in fact—that she'd decided to ignore her attraction to him. She'd had no *idea* then, no idea at all that the attraction she'd felt was mutual. It had been a real shock and just for an instant her blasted hormones had reared up and threatened to take control.

But she'd wrestled them down again. She'd found the strength to do this because, as tempting as it had been to let the kiss go ahead, she'd been right to stop him. She'd been right to decide that she only wanted to be friends with him.

An insistent little voice whispered in her head that 'right' had nothing to do with it. That it was only because she was scared of what might happen, of where the kiss might lead.

She blew out a breath, then crossed to the French doors to let in some air. That annoying voice went on berating her, saying that she should have known that he felt more than friendship for her, that a woman should always know this kind of thing.

Well, maybe other women did, but how was she supposed to know? She had no experience at reading men. She'd never had a relationship with anyone but Shane, and they'd been nothing but kids when they'd met. Over the years, she'd learned to recognise every expression he had in his repertoire, to know what he was thinking at every moment. He'd been her sole focus, until the kids had come along. She'd had no boyfriends before him, and there had certainly been no thoughts of anybody but him during their lengthy marriage.

Ah, but, the pesky little voice whispered, she had known that there was some sort of chemistry between her and Jacques. All those strange physical reactions to him had to have been triggered by something, all those telltale little signs that he'd awoken her dormant femininity had to have been in response to signals he'd given out.

Well, maybe she should have known, but she'd really believed it to be one-sided, a result of her hormones waking from a long, long period of hibernation. She'd never considered that it could be mutual, and when she'd found out she'd panicked, the thought of acting on the attraction too darn scary to contemplate.

She'd never so much as *looked* at another man that way in more than twenty years. And, conversely, there'd never been any reason to believe she was attractive; it had simply never been an issue. She had known her husband loved her regardless of her appearance, and that was all that had ever mattered.

As she'd prepared to come on this trip, she'd never considered the possibility of a man seeing her as anything other than a woman who'd passed her best-before date.

She fanned herself with a postcard she picked up from the table. She'd bought it to send to Sam and Kyle but hadn't had a chance to write it. Was it her imagination or was the night warmer than normal?

Maybe she was having a hot flush? Good timing. Great way to remind herself that she was too old for all this nonsense. She was a middle-aged widow, for heaven's sake!

What would Shane think?

Guilt churned her stomach. Shane would think she was betraying him, that was what.

And she hadn't even done anything yet.

Yet? What did she mean, yet? She wasn't going to do anything.

She moved back to the doors and leaned against the frame while she gazed up at the dark sky. She was used to darker skies and lots of bright stars at home. But she wasn't *at* home. If she were, she'd never have met Jacques and she would never have discovered how naïve she was.

Or how it felt to be told she was attractive. The memory rippled along her nerve endings. She knew it was wrong, but for just a few moments she allowed herself to remember Jacques telling her that she was *very* attractive. A *lovely, vivacious woman*, he'd said. Oh, she knew she shouldn't let it, but the knowledge that he thought so gave her ego a very satisfying stroke.

She hugged herself, rubbing her arms as a cool breeze finally found her overheated skin. Along with his words, she remembered the desire in his eyes when they had rested on her lips. Touching her fingertips to her lips, she tried to imagine what it would have been like to feel his kiss there.

The seconds ticked by, and then she dropped her hand and gave herself a deliberate shake. Time to go back to bed and hopefully, a dreamless sleep.

Jacques pushed Antoine's wheelchair between his mother's lavender and rose bushes. This had become a routine for them on Monday mornings, and Jacques enjoyed it. It was the one day of the week his mother could sleep late, and she deserved the rest after all she did for them. With his brother's help, he took care of Antoine's morning routine, made breakfast, and then he and Antoine spent the remaining time outside having a father-son talk, until it was time for school.

He positioned the wheelchair close to the bench at the end of the garden and sat down. This week, though, he was distracted. When he saw Leonie next, he would apologise to her, and if she forgave him he would be more careful. He had been enjoying her company. She understood when he talked to her about Antoine, and he wanted to be able to do that again.

There was something soothing about her. Perhaps it was her air of calm acceptance. There had been none of that mixture of pity and embarrassment that often filled the eyes of people he talked to about Antoine. Concern, yes, but not pity.

He only knew that when he spent time with her, when he talked to her, he felt as if his world made sense. If he could have chosen a mother for Antoine, he would have wanted someone like Leonie.

Guilt twisted his gut. Familiar guilt. Should he have done more to convince his ex-wife to stay? Maybe counselling would have helped? Or could he have persuaded her to keep in touch at least, so that Antoine would have known his mother?

He'd often wondered whether he'd accepted her departure a little too easily, because it had demanded less effort from him. She had certainly been a demanding person to live with, and married life hadn't been what he'd expected. Whatever he'd done, it had never been good enough for her. As a result, a part of him had been relieved when she'd left.

Antoine's voice broke into his thoughts, and he dragged his mind back to the present, opening his eyes to see his son grinning at him.

'You were asleep.'

'No, I wasn't.'

'What was I talking about, then?'

Jacques hesitated, wondering whether he could bluff his son into believing he'd heard every word, but, no, that wasn't fair, and Antoine deserved his full attention. He sighed. 'I wasn't listening. I'm sorry. Tell me again.'

When Antoine had repeated his story, Jacques smiled, ruffling his son's hair before glancing at his watch. 'It's time for school. We'd better go.'

He wheeled the chair around to the side of the house where the vehicles were parked, and lifted his son into the van. During the drive to school they discussed cars. It was one of their regular subjects, one they shared an interest in, and Jacques had promised his son that he would have a specially adapted car to drive when he was old enough. He would miss out on many of the other pleasures of life as a young man, and Jacques was determined he would not miss out on that one.

Of course, he'd have to be convinced that Antoine was in full and complete control of the vehicle before he'd be allowed out on the road. And he just might have to wait till he was fifty before Jacques decided it was safe.

In the meantime, Antoine devoured motoring magazines, and changed his favourite make of car daily, updating Jacques just as often.

Laughing at Antoine's comments on the new design of an old favourite, Jacques parked the van outside the local school, and went to the back door to unload the wheelchair. Once he'd seen Antoine safely into the school and had a quick chat with his teacher, he drove away, heading back to the vineyard where he'd promised to look over some figures with Bertrand.

Already, he was looking forward to returning to the school later in the day to collect his son. Monday was his favourite day of the week. With the restaurant closed, he had the opportunity to hear Antoine's news while it was still fresh in his mind and he was full of excitement about his day.

He pressed his lips together as he manoeuvred the van along the narrow roads. His son was always cheerful, but was he happy? As much as he had hoped for a stepmother, he'd never known a different way of life, so he couldn't miss it, but Jacques felt as if he'd failed in not providing him with a mother figure.

But after the disappointment of Hélène, who'd taken off after one meeting with his son, he would put neither of them in that position again. There would be no stepmother. For him, the pain of rejection had been magnified many times by seeing his son hurt so badly.

Hélène had been striking with her waist-length black hair and green eyes. The sort of woman any man would be proud to have on his arm, but he'd fallen for the woman he'd thought she was, rather than the woman she turned out to be. And if he were honest, he'd admit that it was not so much losing Hélène that had wounded him, as being robbed of the opportunity for the three of them to live as a family unit.

He'd changed his lifestyle after Hélène. No more girlfriends for him. He didn't have the luxury of making mistakes. Antoine was too important; he needed stability. He did not deserve to be subjected to the ups and downs of his father's dating disasters. If he dated at all now, it was with women who were happy with short-term, casual relationships, which Antoine did not need to know about.

But this brought his thoughts back to Leonie. She was not that type of woman, and he called himself all sorts of names for attempting to kiss her when he'd already known that much about her. Had he frightened her? Had he pushed her too far?

He hoped not, because he intended to make up for his error, if she would let him. He did not want her to fear him making unwanted moves. He wanted her to be able to relax around him. He wanted her to trust him.

She deserved to enjoy her visit. She was a woman who'd never thought of herself, and he envied her husband and family who had bene-fited from her nurturing. He had no doubt she had made them happy, that she would have made their happiness her reason for being. It was time someone thought about making *her* happy.

It would not be him. Not in the long term. Leonie would be leaving at the end of her language course and maybe the temporary nature of this friendship was part of the reason he felt able to open up with her. But if she would speak to him again, he could make her happy for the short time she was here.

What she needed now was company. Someone to talk to. Someone to see the sights with. A friend. He could be the friend she needed.

* * *

A week later, Leonie congratulated herself. By timing her visits to the café to coincide with peak lunchtime, she'd managed to avoid Jacques. She'd received some odd looks from Jean-Claude when he'd served her coffee, as if he thought she was a little crazy, but he hadn't questioned her change of routine, nor the way she shot a wary glance at the door every time it opened. And that was better than changing to another café.

Admittedly, there were plenty to choose from in the fashionable old town, but this one was close to her apartment and she felt comfortable there. Well, she just liked it, she thought with a mental shrug as she dropped the newspaper back in its rack and headed for the door, and she didn't see why she should give it up.

She stood aside to allow an elderly couple to enter and acknowledged their thanks with a smile. She was still smiling when she emerged into the sunlight and saw Jacques leaning against the wall of the building across the street.

Waiting for her.

He had to be. Why else would he be there?

Her stomach had clenched tight at the first sight of him, and when he pushed away from the wall and took the few steps necessary to cross the narrow space her knees turned to water. She hadn't realised how much she missed *seeing* him, actually, physically *seeing* him.

'Leonie.' He spoke softly, and as usual his pronunciation of her name sent a shiver through her. He held out a huge bunch of flowers that she hadn't spotted in his hand, so intent had she been on studying his face.

Predominantly orange, the flowers were so cheerful that she couldn't help smiling again. 'You went to the market.'

'Yes. I remembered that you like bright colours.'

He was right, she did. He always noticed these things about her—was it just her or was he so observant of people in general?

He looked at her with a question in his eyes, and when she took the flowers from him his face showed his relief.

'May I walk with you?'

She dropped her gaze to the flowers and breathed in their sweet scent, giving herself a moment to consider. 'I…I guess so,' she said, exhaling. 'I was going back to the apartment.'

He nodded and turned in that direction with a sigh. 'You've been avoiding me.'

'I haven't.' She winced. What was the point in lying? It was pretty obvious that she had. 'Well, okay, I have.'

'I am sorry that you felt it necessary.' He swore under his breath. 'That makes me feel ashamed. I don't want you to be afraid of me, Leonie.'

'I'm not!' She didn't correct herself this time, because it was true. She'd known as soon as she met him that he was a kind and gentle man, that he was no danger to her safety, but there were other dangers that she hadn't taken into account.

Shaking her head, she said, 'I'm not, really. It's just that I don't want…' She flapped a hand as she struggled to find the right word. She couldn't, even in her own language. 'I don't want *that*.'

Jacques grimaced. He threw up his hands, looking even more French than usual. 'I had no intention of trying to kiss you. It was François and the way he was flirting with you. It made me angry, and…and I am very sorry.'

He looked so remorseful that she bit her lip to stop herself laughing. 'Apology accepted,' she said seriously.

'Do you mean it?'

'Yes.'

'Then, we can forget it ever happened?'

She wasn't so sure about that. She'd tried very hard to forget, but at night she dreamt about Jacques desiring her, repeatedly. She didn't think she could promise to forget.

'I swear that you don't have to worry about it ever happening again.' He shrugged. 'Unless you change your mind.'

'Change my mind?' Her eyes widened, her cheeks heated. 'I won't.'

Jacques tilted his head, and after a moment said, 'Do you think you will ever get over your husband?'

She gasped. 'He's not something I will *get over.* You make him sound like a disease. I don't want to *get over* him. He's part of me, of who I am.'

Holding up his hands in an appeasing gesture, he said, 'I'm sorry, I'm sorry.' He pushed a hand through his hair. 'I don't want to upset you, but I open my mouth and that is what I do. I am an idiot.'

'No, you're not, but you don't understand, and how could you? You haven't been through it. The grief, I mean, and I hope you never have to.'

She moistened her lips. Shane's death had torn a great hole in her life, and that was only right. They'd been together for so long, been through so much together, his loss would always be with her. But it had become much easier to bear in the three years she'd been without him.

'No, I don't understand.' He stopped at the door of her building. 'But I would like to. I would like to know why it is so difficult for you to consider moving on.'

By 'moving on' did he mean being with him in ways that she'd only dreamt about? Oh, goodness, that would mean stepping so far out of her comfort zone, she couldn't even imagine it.

After a deep breath, she gave herself a mental shake. 'I have moved on. I've started to do things I never would have done when Shane was alive, like taking this course.'

'But do you intend to remain alone for the rest of your life?'

She opened her mouth to answer, but the rest of her life suddenly seemed like a very long time. She drew another breath. 'To be honest, I haven't thought that far ahead. I was so comfortable in my relationship with my husband. We had a history together. I knew him, and he knew me. We were used to each other's ways. That sort of relationship takes time to develop.'

'Of course.'

'I don't know whether I have the emotional energy to go through that with someone else.'

She sensed Jacques hesitate, then he went on, 'But not all relationships have to be long term. You don't have to invest that amount of time and energy into a short-term relationship. Sometimes, a casual, passionate relationship can be fun.'

'Fun.' She blushed as she repeated the word. 'I don't know about that,' she said with a shrug. 'I only know that I still feel married to Shane.'

It wasn't true any longer. It hadn't been true for quite some time now, but it sounded final. It would stop Jacques talking about casual, passionate affairs. She didn't want those images in her head. They scared her.

Jacques frowned, and she hurried on.

'Intellectually, I know he's not here anymore, but emotionally I'm as much his wife today as I was on the day he died. I can't be unfaithful to him.'

After a moment's silence, he nodded, and she knew that even though he didn't understand, he would respect her feelings.

'Shall we go for that drive tomorrow, as friends?' he asked, changing the subject.

She gave him a blank look. 'Drive?'

'You wanted to see a *château*, remember? We can go tomorrow if that suits you.'

'Oh! That sounds wonderful, but—'

'There's no need to worry,' he said quickly. 'I won't do anything to make you uncomfortable. You can trust me, I promise.'

'I know. I was only going to say that I didn't want to put you to any trouble, but if you're sure that you don't mind?'

'I'm sure. I know a fantastic place where we can have lunch. The owner is a friend of mine so I know we will be served good food.'

She smiled. 'Sounds great.'

After they'd made arrangements and Jacques had walked away, Leonie went inside and climbed the stairs to her apartment. She'd missed his friendship and hadn't looked forward to spending the rest of her visit alone.

And lonely.

It hit her then that Jacques had been right about her needing to move on. She'd thought she had moved on, but by putting up boundaries and refusing to *feel* again she'd prevented herself from really doing so. And if she didn't do something about that she'd be lonely for the rest of her life, because the kids wouldn't be around for ever. At some stage she'd be alone, and if she let fear stop her from getting involved with anyone else what would her life be like? She didn't even want to think about it.

When she got home she would put more effort into making new friends. Join a club or something. Take up a hobby. The kids would be pleased for her; Sam had been encouraging her to find an interest outside the home for ages now. That was why she'd been so keen on Leonie enrolling for this course, even if it did mean they had to look after themselves for a while.

Inside the apartment, she took out the jug that she'd used as a vase last time, then unwrapped the flowers. But she soon saw that there were far too many to fit in the jug. She wondered what to do. She had so few vessels in the kitchen that she couldn't spare one to do vase duty, and it would pain her to throw out any flowers while they were in their prime.

She paused, tapping her chin as she pondered. When the solution came to her, she separated the bunch into two halves, put one half in water and rewrapped the other. Then she grabbed her handbag and left the apartment again. Outside, she crossed the street, entered the building directly opposite hers and located the door of the apartment that had to be the one. She only hesitated for a moment before knocking, then chewed on her lip until the door opened.

Leonie held out the flowers and introduced herself.

The look on the old lady's face was priceless, but she recovered quickly and beckoned. 'Venez, venez.'

Leonie hadn't expected to be invited in, and she thanked her politely as she stepped over the threshold. After introducing herself as Madame Girard in pretty good English, the woman bustled into the kitchen with the flowers, leaving Leonie standing in the middle of the room. She saw that the apartment was substantially bigger than her own with doors off the main room, as well as the separate kitchen where Madame Girard was running water for the flowers.

She took a step towards the balcony and peered across the street. It was weird to see her temporary home from this angle. Then a picture caught her eye and she turned from the window to take a better look.

It was a photograph of a man of around Madame Girard's age. Dried flowers had been entwined right around the filigree silver frame. Leonie's gaze roamed across several more photos, the same man in various poses, a wedding photograph, in a family group, as a youngster with a football under his arm. A lifetime of memories.

'My husband,' Madame Girard said, placing the vase of flowers behind the photo frame. 'He died.'

After a sympathetic nod, Leonie said, 'My husband died too.'

Madame Girard studied Leonie's face, then made a series of clicking noises with her tongue. She gestured to a pair of armchairs. 'Come. Let us sit and talk.'

Leonie sat, and within minutes discovered that although their experiences were very different, they also had much in common. It felt good to share, and their chat made her realise that she hadn't really talked about the experience of losing her husband to anybody. Not in detail. Not about the effect on her. And as she'd said to Jacques today, no one could understand the grief unless they'd been through it. Madame Girard—Chantal, as she told Leonie to call her—*did* understand.

Eventually, they wept together. Leonie couldn't be sure who'd started to cry first, but they both did their fair share.

It was evening when she crossed the street again. She waved at her new friend, who was watching from the balcony, before she went inside.

She felt different, odd as it seemed to admit it. The stone that had been sitting in her chest since Shane's death was lighter. It was still there, just not as heavy as before. Had talking about his passing helped so much? If she'd known, she'd have done it sooner. Maybe she should have found someone, a grief counsellor perhaps.

She didn't kid herself that she was over his death because she didn't believe she ever would be. Besides, she'd meant it when she'd said she didn't want to get over him. But maybe, just maybe, she would be able to incorporate his absence into her life, and move on.

Carrying the jug of flowers from the kitchen where she'd left it earlier, she placed it in the centre of the small, round dining table. Funny, but on the rare occasions that Shane had bought her flowers they'd been insipid pale pinks or creams, and she'd never said anything because, although she hadn't liked them much, it was the thought that counted, wasn't it? But the flowers that Jacques had bought were exactly to her taste. They were bright; they were full of life.

Jacques was right. It was time she had some fun.

She went back to the kitchen to fetch her simple evening meal of baguette with a soft creamy Brie, then sat at the table where she ate her food, gazed at the flowers and thought about Jacques.

Sitting in his car the next day, Leonie watched as Jacques changed gear. 'It feels strange to be on this side of the car and not have anything to do.'

He flashed her a grin. 'Do you drive much at home?'

'Oh, yes. Or at least, I did when the kids were growing up. They always needed dropping off at one activity or other.'

She smiled to herself. She'd heard other mothers complain about being a free taxi service, but she'd never once objected to all the running around. She'd loved the fact that her children were having so much fun. It had been very different for her, and Shane too. Their parents hadn't encouraged involvement in after-school activities. Partly because of the money; she couldn't deny that the cost of even the cheapest sports and groups soon mounted up. But also, because both of them had been needed at home.

Shane's mum had relied on him to do all the gardening and home maintenance. A little too much, in Leonie's opinion. Shane had been too young to take on some of those jobs, like fixing the leaking roof. It was a job for a professional. But anything she'd said had sounded like a criticism of his mother, which, she'd learned early on, was guaranteed to cause tension between them. So she'd bitten her tongue where his mother was concerned, a habit that had persisted till his mum's sudden death not long after their marriage.

In her own case, she'd taken on the responsibility for all the housework and cooking from an early age. Not so much because her father had asked her to, but because, well, someone had had to do it. And if she hadn't, no one would have done. They'd have lived on takeaway food and the house would have been a tip. She couldn't have lived that way. It had been bad enough having to live with a parent who didn't like her.

Her throat tightened. It still hurt to know that her dad blamed her for the loss of his wife. Growing up without a mother had been hard, but she'd also had to live with the knowledge that every time her father had looked at her, he'd seen the woman he loved in her features and hated her for it.

Before she could stop it, a deep sigh escaped.

'What's wrong?' Jacques' voice was full of concern.

'Oh, I was just remembering things I haven't thought about for a long time.'

'About the children?'

'No.' She looked out of the side window for a moment. When she was sure she wasn't going to cry, she turned back. 'My father. Isn't it silly that we hold onto pain for so long? Even when we've had so much happiness in the meantime, we still remember how much we hurt all those years ago.'

He grimaced. 'A childhood should be as happy as possible. A child should not have to suffer because of its father's mistakes. It is the parent's responsibility to make sure of that, to protect a child from anything that could hurt him.'

'Or her.'

'Yes.' He nodded. 'Or her.'

She was silent, watching his profile as he concentrated on the road ahead. She agreed completely, but she guessed he was thinking of Antoine and blaming himself for the pain the boy had suffered.

She bit her lip. He couldn't have known that two women would walk out on both him and

Antoine. It was not something you could antici-
pate or prepare for. It certainly wasn't his fault.
Her chest ached for his pain.

'If you look over there, you will catch a glimpse
of the battlements of the *château*.'

'Oh.' She put aside all other thoughts for the
moment, and looked in the direction he'd indicated. 'I see it!'

CHAPTER FIVE

HAUT-DE-CAGNES was a fortified medieval town and Leonie was flabbergasted that it had survived. Not only had it survived, but real people were living there. Some of the houses proudly displayed their date of construction as thirteen fifteen, for heaven's sake!

She was fascinated by the little lanes, steps and vaulted passages, and even more so by the total lack of commercialisation. Somehow it had remained unspoilt by tourism. She'd seen only one tourist during their exploration, and that amazed her.

It was so pretty too, with the tightly packed, pale stone houses festooned with vines and other climbing plants, many in full flower.

Then there was the *château*.

'Wow.' She gazed up at its smooth stone walls, well able to believe that Château Grimaldi had withstood many attacks. 'Does anyone live there?'

'No, but it houses several museums so we can go inside if you want to.'

'I do, definitely.'

They climbed the steps to the ticket office at the main entrance, then wandered around the olive-tree museum on the ground floor where they also found exhibits about life in the medieval castle.

'I'm so glad we came here,' Leonie said as they moved around the next floor and the museum of modern art.

'If you like this, you should like Nice. It has more galleries and museums than anywhere else outside Paris.'

'Really? I must make an effort to see some of them. Who knows? I might even learn something about art.'

He shrugged. 'The main thing to learn is that it should make you happy to look at it.'

'Yes. Good point.'

They walked on and she gazed up at a spectacular, *trompe-l'oeil* ceiling. 'Look at that. This place is fantastic.'

He nodded. 'Not all *châteaux* are like this one, of course. Some are much smaller and not so old.'

'Are there any that are still lived in?'

'Oh, yes. Some are now inhabited by movie stars, Hollywood royalty you could say, and other celebrities. Others are still owned by the family that built them, several generations ago. We will have lunch at one of these later. My friend has converted part of the *château* into a hotel.'

She did a double take. Jacques was standing with his arms folded and, with the *château* wall as a backdrop, she could readily imagine him as a medieval knight. As a knight in shining armour.

She smothered a sigh. What a silly, romantic thought. This wasn't like her. She'd always been practical, not romantic.

Later, they made their way back to the car and just like that morning, Leonie's heart seemed to speed up at the prospect of sitting in the small space with Jacques, the fragrance of his cologne wrapping around her.

Giving herself a mental shake, she decided she'd better get her blood pressure tested when she returned to Australia. She was at the age when all sorts of things needed to be checked, and an abnormal heartbeat was more likely to be caused by age than by being alone in the car with Jacques. Wasn't it?

But although she told herself not to be so stupid, once the doors were closed she couldn't help breathing in his scent as if she couldn't get enough of it.

Jacques' friend's *château* was wonderful. They were sitting outside on a simple terrace, sipping champagne that their host had insisted on opening to celebrate their visit. He'd gone off to give special instructions to the kitchen so she expected to be in for another treat when the food arrived.

He'd shown them around the *château* before leaving them alone on the terrace, and she'd been very impressed by the attention to detail in its decoration, even those rooms that were for guests. Every room was huge, dressed with sumptuous fabrics, furnished with what she assumed to be antique pieces, and had a chic bathroom with every modern convenience.

A light breeze fluttered the leaves of a stand of magnificent old trees near the terrace, as well as Leonie's hair. She pushed it back from her face while she gazed up at the *château* with its five windows across each of three floors.

'It's quite different from Château Grimaldi,' she said.

'Centuries apart,' Jacques replied.

'Yes, but it's beautiful.' She turned to face the extensive park with an elaborate fountain in the foreground. 'The grounds are beautiful too. I imagine they'd do almost anything to make sure it stays in the family.'

'Yes, that's the reason for the hotel.'

'It must have hurt to have to turn the family home into a business.'

They weren't the only couple on the terrace, but the tables were separated by quite a distance so she wasn't worried about being overheard.

'It's not so bad. It has provided employment for local people, and ensured the financial viability of the *château*. And they're sociable people, not protective of their privacy like some.'

As she took another sip from her glass soft fingers of sunlight reached through the leaves of the trees and touched the crisp white tablecloth. It was an idyllic setting. And that thought was followed by a sense of wonder. That she was here. In France. Sitting on the terrace of a *château*. About to have lunch with the sexiest man she'd ever known.

She stilled as she took it all in. Was she the same woman who, a short time ago, had never been further than two hours' drive from the house where she'd grown up? Whose most exciting moments had been those experienced by her children? Who had never even thought of a man as sexy, never mind had lunch with him?

Their first course was delivered, jerking her back to the present, and she pushed her sunglasses to the top of her head to look at the colourful food on her plate. 'Is that ratatouille?'

He nodded. 'Provence is where it originated.'

'I didn't know that.' She tasted a mouthful and

smiled. Several moments later, she said, 'What about your family, Jacques? Where are you from?'

'My family home is a vineyard.'

'A vineyard! Goodness, that's where you live?'

'Yes, with Antoine, my mother and my brother, as I said before.'

'Where is it?'

'It's about fifty minutes from Nice, in what we call the Arrière-Pays.'

Leonie didn't try to retain the details of its location. It wasn't as if she'd ever have to drive there, and she found his description of the landscape far more interesting. She liked the sound of the rugged mountains, steep canyons and fast-flowing rivers.

'Why do you work in Nice? Aren't you needed at the vineyard?'

He shook his head. 'For one thing, the restaurant is my responsibility. Mine alone. My grandfather left it to me because he knew that I loved it. And I am determined to make sure it lives up to his vision for it so I don't intend to hand it over to someone else to manage.'

She nodded. 'I can understand that.'

'But also, the vineyard is my brother's domain and he runs it the way he wants to—which is not the way I would want to. We have tried to work together, but—' he gave a rueful shrug '—we can't do it. So, we agreed to disagree. We both own the vineyard, but he manages it.'

'Don't you get on?'

'As brothers, yes. As business partners, no. We're too…I don't know, like lions.'

Her eyes widened. 'Lions?'

Laughing, he said, 'You know, when those nature documentaries show a pride of lions, the most senior lion is always challenged by the second-in-line and has to chase him off. That is what we are like, Bertrand and me.'

'You both want to be head of the pride.' She smiled at the image of the two brothers, butting heads to be the alpha male. Oh, wait, she thought, that was stags not lions. Lions would go for each other's throats. No, no, no, she couldn't see Jacques as a lion. He was far too nice. Strong, yes, she could believe that, but not vicious.

'I take it he is the eldest?'

He nodded.

'Couldn't you curb your need to challenge your brother for Antoine's sake?'

He grimaced. 'It wouldn't work. Let's just say, it's better for us to live and work apart.'

'I see.' Pity, she thought, but it wasn't her place to question his family's dynamics. Come to think of it, would Sam and Kyle be able to work together if the opportunity arose? Probably not. Kyle would soon drive his sister mad.

'Do you ever get sick of commuting?'

'Not really.' He shook his head as he leaned back to allow the waiter to present him with a plate of chicken topped with a bright green herb sauce.

'Anyway, I have a villa in Nice. I stay there when I need to, when I know I'm going to be late, or…for other reasons.' He stopped to take a drink from his wine glass.

When he was dating and wanted to take a woman to bed? She reached for her glass too, wishing she hadn't had that thought.

Clearing her throat, she said, 'Do you have any other brothers and sisters, or just Bertrand?'

'No, he's the only one.'

'And did you get on well as you were growing up?'

'Yes. We had our fights as brothers do, but we had a good time.' He grinned, and in the dappled light of the terrace, with his white teeth and gleaming eyes, he looked like a man from a fantasy.

Or a dream.

She swallowed, her own latest dream vivid in her memory. She shivered, but the goose bumps on her forearms were not caused by the gentle breeze drifting over her skin. She told herself all the reasons why she shouldn't see him in any light other than friendship. Reminded herself who she was, and why she was here.

But still, she couldn't deny the ripple of awareness that was turning her insides to jelly.

Maybe…

No. She couldn't think about it. Couldn't even consider it.

Dessert provided the distraction she needed. A sweet tart crammed with strawberries and served with swirls of two sauces, one vanilla and the other rich chocolate.

She closed her mouth over a forkful and moaned with pleasure. As she opened her eyes the smile froze on her lips. Jacques was looking at her as if he found her more delicious than the dessert.

No man had ever looked at her that way before and it both frightened and thrilled her.

He recovered quickly, and began a light-hearted account of the trouble he and his brother had managed to get into as kids, his intention, clearly, being to pretend that the look had never happened, perhaps hoping that she hadn't noticed.

But she had noticed. And she didn't think she would ever be able to forget.

That night Leonie dreamed of Jacques again. This time when she woke she lay still, not wanting to move in case doing so would chase away the incredible sense of warmth and of joy that had filled her dream world and lingered once her eyes had opened.

How could a dream feel so real? Real enough that her body still throbbed with desire.

She hardly knew how she'd be able to look at Jacques when she saw him again, knowing what they'd been doing in her imagination. The details were no longer sharp, but she remembered enough to be embarrassed.

Eventually, and languidly, she rolled over and swung her feet to the ground. If she continued like this she was going to look all of her forty-plus years and more. She couldn't get by on a few short hours of sleep a night without it showing in her face.

She paused in the act of opening the fridge. She was becoming vain in her old age, she thought. She'd never cared before about the crow's feet or the smile lines.

She plonked herself down at the little table and drank some water. She didn't know what bothered her most: having sensual dreams about a man, or the fact that she was starting to wonder whether the real thing would be as good as the dream version, and whether she'd ever find out.

Groaning, she dropped her forehead to the table. This was no good. Somehow, she had to return to the mindset where she didn't even *think* about sex. With anyone. If she didn't, she'd go crazy. Why had these niggling little doubts and questions entered her head now, when she'd been so definite about her wish to be no more than friends such a short time ago?

She thought she knew why. Something Jacques had said had lodged itself in her brain. His comment about fun. That, combined with her newly discovered and uncontrollable hormones, and growing curiosity about how different sex might be with him, had sent her subconscious into overdrive.

Well, it had to stop. She needed her sleep, and her peace of mind. And she needed to be able to look Jacques in the eye.

Over the next week, Leonie and Jacques settled into a pattern. He left the restaurant as soon as the lunch rush was over, sometimes even earlier, and they spent the afternoon together, seeing the sights of Nice while she expanded her vocabulary by learning new French words every day.

She learned a lot about Jacques at the same time. She discovered that he knew many people around Nice, and they all seemed to regard him highly. She had to concentrate to keep up with the conversations that they fell into wherever they went. It was either learn quickly, or be left out.

Not that Jacques would ever let her be excluded if he could help it, but his friends and acquaintances weren't always so considerate.

He showed her some of those museums and galleries he'd mentioned. She enjoyed the Matisse museum; the simplicity of his paintings touched her.

He took her out of the city to Cap Ferrat, a resort for the rich and famous where they drove past high hedges and gates protecting villas that were once inhabited by people like Édith Piaf and the Duke and Duchess of Windsor.

Leonie's eyes were already wide when they arrived at the Musée Ephrussi de Rothschild, the rose-pink villa created by Béatrice, a member of the famous banking family. She'd amassed countless pieces of priceless art, along with an impressive collection of antique furniture and rare porcelain.

Leonie was a little overwhelmed by the sheer size of the collections and the lavishness of the villa's décor, although she did enjoy the little room that was decorated by paintings of dancing monkeys. They were cute. And she particularly liked Béatrice's boudoir, complete with a writing desk that had been owned by Marie-Antoinette. But most of all she loved the grounds with their themed gardens, the main one modelled on the deck of a ship.

'Apparently, Béatrice employed extra staff to wander around here in sailors' uniforms,' Jacques said, laughing. 'Can you imagine it?'

'Not really.' She grinned. She'd given up apologising for occupying his time because he appeared to be enjoying himself just as much as her.

She took off her sunglasses and turned to look back at the pink house. Her cotton skirt brushed the lavender border around the ornamental pool and she sniffed as its scent drifted up to her.

'It's hard to imagine this as a family home. I mean, I can't see teenagers dropping school bags on the floor, or having friends over.'

'Well, it wasn't Béatrice's main home, and she didn't have children.'

'Right.' She nodded, wondering if Béatrice had been lonely. 'I suppose she had to do something with her spare time, then.' Although she felt sure *she* could have come up with better things to do with so much time and money, but thank goodness she hadn't had to. She'd had Sam and Kyle, and Shane. It was good to have other people to think about, to be needed. She suddenly felt sorry for Béatrice.

In between all this art and culture, Jacques had been educating her on the local food specialities and they'd eaten snacks at pavement cafés, or picnicked in the city's parks. She'd tried bouillabaisse and beignets, *pan bagnat*—a sandwich filled with salad Niçoise—and her favourite, *pissaladière,* a sort of combination of quiche and pizza.

The next day, Saturday, he insisted she had to try *socca,* a kind of pancake made from chickpea flour and olive oil, sprinkled with lots of black pepper and eaten with the fingers.

They sat at a table outside the brasserie where he'd bought it, sharing a large plate of golden *socca.*

'You're full of good ideas,' she said, reaching for another piece just as he did too.

Their fingers bumped and Leonie's stomach leapt into her throat, her mind instantly flying to the way he'd touched her in her dreams.

'I'm sorry. You first.' He smiled as he gestured for her to go ahead.

She giggled—she actually giggled—as she tried again, this time managing to take a piece of *socca* from the plate. She was behaving like a teenager with a crush on a boy, and she didn't know what to do about it.

One idea flashed into her head.

She couldn't. But, oh, her cheeks grew hot just thinking about putting an end to her speculation.

'So, how's the course going?'

She dragged her mind back from unfamiliar territory. 'Much better. It's amazing how much of the language I've picked up just from spending time with you, and now that I've caught up with the other students I'm finding it much easier.'

She still felt she should be warning them to be careful when they went out at night, but she'd managed to bite her lip and not sound too much like their mother. They had relaxed around her too, so the classes were more enjoyable than they had been in the early days. But she reckoned she'd actually learned a great deal more from being around Jacques.

'So, you're glad you stayed?'

'Oh, yes. I like it here, very much.' She sighed. 'It's almost a pity I have to go home.'

He eyed her for a moment. 'You would consider living here?'

'Oh, no. No, I said "almost". I'm definitely going home. Well, I couldn't stay.' She shrugged. 'My home is where my kids are, so it's not even an issue. For as long as they need me, I will be there for them.'

'Of course.' He took a bite of *socca* and chewed it. He looked away for a long moment, then turned back and asked, 'Will you come to lunch at La Bergamote tomorrow?'

She hesitated for a moment, before agreeing. 'Yes, that would be lovely. Thank you.'

She hadn't eaten there since Jacques had told

her he found her attractive. Her stomach bubbled and fizzed as she recalled the moment when she'd thought he was going to kiss her. What would have happened if she hadn't panicked and rushed away? Well, obviously, he would have kissed her, but how would he have tasted? How would his lips have felt on hers?

After all the time she'd spent wondering, she'd love the chance to find out. She wasn't even sure that if the same thing happened tomorrow, she would still stop him.

Shock took her breath for a moment. Would she really take the chance if it were offered again? Thoughts and emotions tumbled over each other while she tried to work out where she was going with this.

She was pretty sure that this powerful attraction she felt was not simply a case of her hormones putting in an appearance after all these years. She liked him, really *liked* him, and she was profoundly curious to know what it would be like to be kissed by him.

Was that wrong? A little while ago, she would have said that it was. But now? She wasn't so sure.

But, of course, it wouldn't happen again. Their relationship was on a firm footing now. There was no ambiguity. Jacques had promised a platonic friendship, and she knew he would honour his promise. It was almost a pity that he had so much integrity, she thought, and then rolled her eyes at her own irrational thoughts.

After leaving Jacques, and before she went back to her apartment, Leonie selected several of the beautifully displayed marzipan fruits that she'd spotted in a small shop window. She watched the shop assistant pack them into a small white box and tie it up with delicate pink ribbon. The French certainly knew about presentation, she thought as she took the box with a smile. They would even put a couple of cookies in a box and decorate it with an elegant bow.

On the way back to her street, her thoughts turned to Jacques. No surprise there, she thought. She couldn't seem to stop thinking about him. Day or night.

She knocked on Chantal's apartment door and, when the door opened, handed over the pretty little box.

Chantal's face lit up—at the gift or the company, Leonie wasn't sure. After having been invited inside, Leonie followed her into the kitchen where she made them both a drink using peppermint syrup and Perrier from the fridge. The bright green drink was cool and refreshing and just what Leonie needed.

When they were seated in the main room, she told Chantal about the sightseeing she'd been doing with Jacques, describing in detail the places she'd enjoyed the most.

'Huh, you've been busy.'

'Yes, it's been all go.'

'He is handsome, your young man.'

Leonie's hand jerked. 'Oh, he's not mine,' she said hastily. He was handsome, she couldn't argue with that. She chuckled and said, 'He's not young either.'

Chantal gave Leonie a sideways look. 'To me, you are both young,' she said, then sighed heavily. 'I remember being your age and, no, I didn't think I was young at the time. But now I look back and think, I was.'

'I don't feel young. Maybe because so much has happened in my life.'

'Yes.' Chantal reached across to pat her hand. 'Much of what has happened to you is bad. Now you should have some fun. It is time.'

Jacques' image flashed into her head. She recalled his idea of fun—a casual relationship, and a passionate one. Not what Chantal meant, of course. She cleared her throat. 'I am having, um, fun. It's been good seeing so much of the city, and—'

Chantal cut her off with the clicking of her

tongue that Leonie had come to know well. 'That's not what I mean by fun. I am sure you can find something better to do with such a good-looking man than sightseeing. And better than sitting alone at night, over there.' She nodded towards Leonie's window.

Her cheeks grew hot, but she kept a straight face. 'Jacques is busy at night, that's when he works. And anyway, I'm not really into…night-life.'

Chantal rolled her eyes. 'I know you miss your husband. I do too, but it's different for me. I'm an old woman. You still have good years ahead of you. Don't waste them.'

After a moment's silence, Leonie asked, 'Do you ever go shopping?'

'Of course. I buy my food on alternate mornings.'

'What about shopping for clothes? You are always dressed so immaculately.'

'I have a room full of classic outfits. I do not need to buy more.'

'But you know where to go for nice clothes?'

'Why? Are you going to improve the way you dress?'

Leonie winced. 'I think so. I'd like something nice to wear tomorrow when I go to Jacques' restaurant.'

Chantal gave a satisfied nod. 'Good. You dress like a child.'

'I do?' Leonie wasn't sure whether to be offended. 'I like comfortable clothes.'

Chantal clucked. 'You have no style. This…' She waved a hand at Leonie's full skirt. 'This is not attractive to a man.'

'Well, I haven't been trying to be attractive to a man.' Until now. She shook off the thought. 'I just want to look more—' she shrugged '—more stylish.'

'Come.' Chantal stood. 'I know exactly where to take you.'

Leonie recalled Chantal's advice that she should have some fun later when she was getting into bed. It was easy for her to say, she thought. Of course, *she* would probably say the same herself to someone else, but it was one thing giving that type of advice, and quite another taking it.

She lay in bed wide awake and wondering. Wondering whether she should have sex with Jacques and put an end to this intense yearning that just wouldn't quit. She'd gone from a surprising attraction with no thought of anything more than friendship, to a full-blown desperate need to feel his body pressed against hers.

She couldn't go on like this. She had to do

something decisive, or lose her sanity. She was suffering from a hormonal overload, and if she didn't do something about it she would go mad. Maybe she'd gone mad already. Maybe that was why she was thinking this way. Because she certainly wasn't in her right mind.

She snapped her head from one side to the other. Of course she wouldn't do it. She couldn't. What if she disappointed him? What if he didn't like her ageing body? It would ruin their friendship and leave her feeling worse than she did now.

Some time later, she was still hovering on the brink of sleep when she suddenly jackknifed upright. She hadn't thought about Shane all day.

Not once.

She hadn't even thought of him amongst the reasons she couldn't sleep with Jacques. Did this mean she'd accepted that it was time to move on?

She remembered reading that death forced you to look back, while acceptance involved slowly turning around and looking forwards. She hadn't completely understood it at the time, but now she felt she'd been turning slowly since she'd first met Jacques.

CHAPTER SIX

AT LA BERGAMOTE the next day, Jacques glanced at Leonie, not sure what was different about her, but something was. She hadn't changed her hair, which was still a mass of blond curls that looked as soft as cotton wool. How would it feel to bury his fingers in them?

He gave himself a shake. He couldn't let himself think like that or his mind would run away with him. Much safer not to notice how sexy she looked in her silver-grey dress. Maybe that was it? He hadn't seen the dress before and, now he came to think of it, it wasn't her usual style.

She normally wore skirts or shorts with T-shirts, and it was a look that suited her. Sweet and homely. But this dress suited her too. His breath caught for a moment as he checked her out. It was a much more tailored look and it showed off her curvaceous shape.

He hoped François didn't drop in today. He did

not want to have to sit by and watch him devour her with his eyes again.

'You look very nice, Leonie.'

'Oh. Thank you.'

He could have sworn she was blushing. 'Is that a new dress?'

'Yes. I felt out of place last time I was here, so I went out and bought this.'

He frowned, hating the thought that she'd felt out of place in his restaurant. He certainly wouldn't have guessed that she did. She'd seemed perfectly at ease as always.

That was it. That was the difference today. She was nervous.

But why?

'I bought shoes too.' She flapped a hand towards her feet. 'Gosh, they're killing me. I haven't worn heels in…oh, I can't remember the last time I did. Too many years ago.'

She took a deep breath and his eyes dipped to the lower-than-normal neckline of her dress as her chest rose and fell. Snapping his gaze away, he drew in a deep breath of his own, then gestured to the rear of the restaurant. 'Would you like to see the kitchen?'

She nodded. 'That would be great.'

'This way.' He touched her back, and thought he heard her gasp. 'Are you okay? Are those shoes really hurting your feet?'

'No. Yes. I mean, they are, but I'm okay.'

In the kitchen, he guided Leonie to a spot from where she could watch the preparations without being in the way, then he crossed to his head chef. He brought Philippe back with him and made the introductions.

Leonie told Philippe how much she'd enjoyed the food on her previous visit and, gratified, the chef told her how happy he was to have a beautiful woman visit his kitchen.

Leonie blushed. Again. Jacques felt there was something he didn't understand. Something that had happened. Something he'd missed.

'Goodness, you have…what, seven chefs working for you? You must be very organised.'

Philippe shrugged. 'They all know their jobs.'

'Yes, they all look very intent on what they're doing.'

They chatted for a few moments more, then Philippe excused himself to take care of an urgent task. Jacques escorted Leonie out of the kitchen and to a table where he made sure she was comfortable before leaving to check with his maître d' that all was under control.

Leonie watched Jacques walk away from the table, then let out the breath she'd been holding. She hoped he hadn't noticed anything strange about her behaviour, but she just couldn't seem to act naturally. She felt twitchy and out of her depth.

It was bad enough that he'd noticed the way she looked. Not that she didn't like her new dress. She wasn't used to such a figure-hugging style, and low neckline, but she did like it. But why had she let Chantal talk her into wearing such a sexy outfit?

The reason was that she'd wanted Jacques to look at her and see the woman he'd found attractive, not the friend he'd been spending so much companionable time with. And the look in his eyes before he'd been able to hide it had told her that the attraction was still there. It seemed she was learning to read his dark eyes after all, because she'd caught a glimpse of the hunger and the heat.

It wasn't as if she'd decided to throw herself at him. All she'd decided to do was consider the *possibility* that she *might* change her mind about the kind of relationship she wanted.

Oh, who was she trying to kid? If there was any chance of regaining her sanity, of ever sleeping again, she was going to have to…well, kiss him, at least. She couldn't think beyond that.

Now, how to let him know that she'd changed her mind about the type of relationship she wanted?

She was a grown woman, for heaven's sake.

She shouldn't have a problem with this. Groaning, she sipped the water that had been awaiting her on the table. She could just come right out and say it, she supposed. That was probably the best way to approach the subject and she'd always preferred being straightforward. But her mouth dried at the thought of speaking the words.

He was heading her way, so she took a deep breath and straightened her spine. Involuntarily, one hand went to her hair, but there was little point, her curls never looked any different.

'Thanks for showing me the kitchen,' she said as he sat down. 'I've never actually been inside a restaurant kitchen before.'

He smiled. 'You're welcome, any time.'

She gazed at him, taking in the gleam in his eyes, the creases around them, his mouth…oh, his mouth. She swallowed. 'Jacques, I…'

'Yes?' He looked away, catching the eye of the waiter who was at their table in an instant, then turned back and gave her his full attention.

'Oh, nothing.' She couldn't blurt it out now, with the waiter there. In fact, she didn't know whether she could do it at all. What was she thinking? This was not her. She didn't flirt with gorgeous men in foreign countries. Nor anywhere else, for that matter.

Soon, she'd return home to take care of Sam

and Kyle, and she'd forget all about Jacques and his dazzling smile and…and he was still looking at her as if he expected her to say something.

'I'm hungry. That's all.'

Grinning, he said, 'You're in the right place, then. We can do something about that.'

'Yes.' She bit her lip. Okay, she had to focus on something else. Food would do for a start.

By the time they'd ordered, she had decided she wasn't going to say or do anything at all about changing her mind. It was easier to stay as they were. Friends. No complications. Going slowly insane in private was not as bad as proposition-ing Jacques would have been.

Her decision made it much easier to relax into conversation and the time went quickly, even though they lingered over the meal.

Over the next few days, Jacques took her further afield—to Grasse, where they visited a perfume factory and she had the thrill of creating her own perfume; to Cannes, where she was amazed when Jacques told her the glorious sandy beach was made from imported sand covering the natural pebbles; and to St Tropez, where she was charmed by the pastel-painted fishermen's houses clustered around the old port, and by the traditional fishing boats moored alongside luxury yachts in the port itself.

At the end of Saturday's trip, Jacques invited her back to his home for coffee.

She looked up, swallowed and said, 'Coffee would be lovely.'

She hoped she sounded natural, but her heart was thumping when Jacques turned off the road in the stylish and hilly Cimiez district, north of the city. And this was just at the prospect of seeing where he lived. How would her poor heart have coped if he'd suggested more?

'The Villa Broussard,' she read from the sign on the stone pillar marking his gateway. 'How creative.' She shot him a quick grin. 'Was that the best you could do?'

'Well, it avoids confusion if nothing else.' He parked the car, then came around to open her door.

She gazed at the boxy white building as she got out, reserving judgement as to whether she liked it or not, but as soon as she entered the bright and sunny home she was sold.

After he'd shown her through the main rooms, which were decorated in a classic, timeless style, Jacques made coffee and they sat on the broad, balustraded terrace. Gazing at the wonderful view south over the slopes of a park and then the city, they settled into a comfortable, companionable silence, the only sounds the whistling of birds and chirping of insects. She didn't need to be racing all over the Côte d'Azur to enjoy herself with Jacques. This was enough. Just being with him made her happy.

She glanced across at him. It wasn't just the way he looked, but everything about him. Shadows fluttered over his face as a breeze moved the spreading branches of a tree above the terrace. She could stay there all day—or what was left of it. She let the warmth of the sun seep into her bones and relaxed more completely than she could ever remember doing.

Later, through almost-closed eyes, she became aware of Jacques checking his watch and she roused herself. 'That time already?'

He gave her a rueful smile. 'I'm sorry, I didn't mean to wake you.'

'You didn't. I wasn't sleeping, only resting. So, is it time to go?'

'I'm afraid so.' He stood and crossed to the side of her chair where he held out a hand to help her up.

Hyper-aware of his hand's warmth and of its strength when it closed around hers, she got to her feet, then surprised herself by not letting go.

A reaction flickered in his eyes. She didn't know what it was. She hadn't fully learned to read them yet, but that was okay. She didn't have to know everything about him. As he'd said, not all relationships had to be long term. She wasn't looking for someone to replace Shane; she wanted a new experience, one that she had never had before.

She lifted her free hand to his face, feeling the slight roughness of its skin beneath her palm. A muscle jerked in his cheek, his eyes darkened. She'd surprised him, she could see that.

'Kiss me, Jacques.'

His lips parted in shock. He stepped back, out of reach of her hands. 'No, Leonie, no. You don't want this. I promised.'

'But I do.' She reached for him again, her hands on either side of his face. 'I've changed my mind.'

His breath rushed out in a gasp. 'What?'

'You said if I changed my mind…remember? Well, I have. I want to have some fun. With you.'

'Ah, *mon Dieu.*' He shook his head, mumbling something in French that she couldn't decipher. 'But why? You were so certain. What has made you change your mind?'

She was sure he'd see the beating of her heart through her T-shirt. 'I guess it's a combination of things. I don't want to go home without knowing what it's like to kiss you. I've been…' She couldn't tell him how she'd lain awake at night fantasising about him. 'I've been wondering what it would be like.'

His eyes had narrowed, and they seemed to

bore into her, as if he were trying to see what was inside her head. 'What you are saying is that you want to kiss, but that is all. Yes?'

'No…I mean, I don't know.' She shrugged, at a loss to explain. 'I don't think so. I think I want one of those passionate relationships you talked about, but how can I be sure until I take the first step?'

He sighed. 'Leonie, have you thought about this? You said you wouldn't be unfaithful to your husband. You said you felt you were still married.'

'I know.' She frowned, remembering the words that had been intended to put him off. 'But I believe I was meant to meet you, that you were meant to show me that I'm still alive.'

He lifted his head, and looked at her the way no man had ever looked at her before. His gaze roamed all over her, making her feel exposed and desired and…oh, she was turning to jelly.

When his gaze finally locked with hers, a wave of longing travelled down her spine and spread through her pelvis. She could feel the rush of blood in her thighs. She'd been having sex for more than twenty years, yet she'd never known this explosion of desire.

'I can do that,' he said at last. 'But I don't want to hurt you.'

'I know we're not talking about long term, Jacques. I'm not stupid.'

'No, of course you're not.'

'I'd like some fun. Just for a short time. Just until I go home and step back into my normal life. This way, my kids don't need to know. I wouldn't dream of doing something like this around them.'

He stepped forward, took hold of her shoulders and lightly touched his lips to hers.

Her eyes widened when he pulled back. Was that all?

But his eyes were asking her a question. She saw it and recognised it for what it was. She swallowed, then moistened her lips. 'Yes, I do mean it, Jacques.'

He kissed her with all the passion she could have wanted. His mouth drifted over hers, he traced her lips with his tongue, then coaxed them apart. All the questions she'd asked herself, all the debates she'd been having with herself, the constant back-and-forth, should-she-shouldn't-she, ended in that one exhilarating moment.

He gathered her into his arms as she sank into him, savouring his taste, inhaling his warm, masculine scent, feeling the heat of his body and the strength of his arms encircling her. His kiss sparked into life parts of her that had been dormant for a very, very long time.

Finally, they leaned against each other. Leonie could feel Jacques' heart beating every bit as hard as her own, and it flattered and reassured her.

'Are you okay?' he said eventually.

'Better than okay.' She lifted her head from his shoulder, smiling. 'I liked it. I liked it a lot.'

'Me too.' He sighed, then smiled. 'A lot.' He pushed his fingers into her hair and sighed again. 'So soft. I've wanted to do this for so long.'

It felt so intimate, his fingertips on her scalp and brushing the nape of her neck as he lifted her hair and breathed kisses behind her ear. Leonie cleared her throat. 'Had we better go now?'

'Yes.' He brought his eyes back to her face. 'But…soon…'

His voice trailed off, but his eyes burned. She knew what he'd left unsaid and it made her tingle all over.

CHAPTER SEVEN

WHAT did you wear when you were in your forties and going on your first date?

Leonie had no idea, but she was determined to find something suitable. It might help if she knew where they were going on their date, but Jacques hadn't elaborated.

She didn't want to wear black. It reminded her of Shane's funeral, which was the last time she'd worn it. Anything but that. She headed straight for the shop that Chantal had taken her to, and that was where she found the dress. The one. A wraparound knee-length dress in a shimmering kingfisher blue. It made her feel feminine, even attractive, and would be appropriate for almost any venue.

The dress was flattering, without a doubt. It showed off her good bits and covered up the not-so-good. Which brought to mind something that had been bothering her ever since she'd told Jacques she'd changed her mind.

What would he think of her body?

It was okay when covered and disguised, especially by a dress as cleverly designed as this one. But without clothes?

Between gravity and childbirth, her body was wrecked. Well, okay, not exactly wrecked, but it definitely showed the effects of every one of her years.

She regretted now that she'd never bothered with the toning exercises they advocated in all those glossy magazines. But there had never been any point. Only one man had ever seen her naked and he was the father of the children who'd caused the stretch marks and other signs of motherhood. He'd had no problem with them.

But she remembered Jacques saying that French people liked to look at beautiful things, and she wasn't at all confident that her body would live up to his expectations.

Well, there was only one course of action— and it wasn't to back out now. No, she'd just have to make sure the lights were out. Darkness would be her ally.

Letting out the breath she'd been holding, she changed into her usual clothes, then took the dress to the sales assistant. The smiling woman happily dealt with her purchase, even bringing to her attention some coordinated shoes and a filmy wrap which Leonie also bought. And when, blushing, Leonie enquired about underwear, the assistant was only too happy to help with that too. Consequently, Leonie now owned her first set of sexy lingerie. First set of matching underwear of any type actually, never mind sexy.

Goodness, she'd never spent so much money on clothes, she thought as she left the store. In her entire married life, she'd never owned a single item of clothing that made her feel as good as this new dress did, and she had to admit the lacy bra and panties had an effect too. A very different feeling from the sensible cotton knickers and sturdy bra she was used to.

When she spotted a beauty salon, she only hesitated for a moment before entering. She might as well go all the way and look as good as she could.

Despite her conviction that she was not going to back out, her heart was slamming against her ribs when she saw Jacques from her apartment window on Sunday evening. And it didn't slow when she hurried down the stairs to meet him. She'd been alone with him many times, but this time seemed different.

It *was* different. It was the first time they'd been on a date.

In contrast to her, he looked relaxed and sure

of himself. He was perfectly comfortable while she had a case of nerves that made her stomach churn and her throat constrict.

She joined him in the street, and then she had the satisfaction of seeing him look less than relaxed. His stunned eyes didn't leave her as she closed the door and made her way to his side.

'You look… You look…'

'Okay?'

'No.' He shook his head. 'Much, much better than okay. You are stunning. Very, very beautiful.'

Never in her life had she provoked such a reaction from a man. The thrill of it made her stand a little taller in her high heels, and pull her shoulders back a little further. For a moment, she couldn't speak, her throat was so tight with the knowledge that *this* man thought she was beautiful. And he wasn't just paying her an empty compliment. She could see the truth in the way his eyes caressed her.

Leonie settled the wrap around her shoulders and smiled as her voice returned. 'It's the dress. I'm glad you like it.'

'The dress is very nice. But without you, it would just be a piece of fabric. You make it…perfect.'

She beamed at him, then she heard a voice above her and turned to wave at Chantal who was smiling and nodding from her balcony. Evidently, she approved too—of the dress or of Jacques, or both.

Jacques felt very proud to have Leonie on his arm as they walked through the old town. She'd clearly gone to some trouble with her appearance and the results were sensational. Curls tumbled from the top of her head in a style that looked about to fall down, but which, he guessed, was a deliberate effect. Her dress was eye-catching, but the body inside it fascinated him. She wasn't big, but she had curves that filled out the dress to perfection.

He'd always liked the way she looked, but the thought that she'd made this effort for him made him suck in a breath. He looked at her hand on his arm, then covered it with his other hand, looking forward to the evening he'd planned.

They started with an aperitif on the Cours Saleya, followed by a sumptuous dinner at a luxury hotel, then moved on to a club, one of the few where you could actually have a conversation at the bar. With sleek décor, a piano bar and a dance floor with a live band, it attracted a smart crowd aged between twenty-five and fifty. Just right for the two of them.

Sitting on a bar stool, Leonie seemed to be having difficulty keeping her dress together. At the least movement, it separated, slithering over her legs and revealing her thighs. And very attractive thighs they were too.

In another woman, the move might have been deliberate, but Leonie kept pulling the edges together in a self-conscious way. Because he thought she seemed uncomfortable, and because the sight of her legs was making him impatient to feel her in his arms, he asked her to dance.

She agreed. 'But it's been a long, long time since I danced,' she said with a rueful smile. 'I'll probably make a complete mess of it.'

He shrugged. 'I won't care, as long as I can hold you while you do it. You've been tempting me all evening in that dress.'

She laughed, that genuine, sunny laugh that he associated with her, then she stepped into his arms and he was forced to notice her softness, to acknowledge how perfectly her body fitted against his, to recognise the rightness of everything about this picture.

He drew her closer with a sigh. Dancing was, by far, one of his better ideas. One tune blended into another, and then another before he leaned his mouth close to her ear and said, 'Let's get out of here.'

In response to her nod, he put an arm around her shoulders, half-protective, half-possessive. He had an overwhelming need to let everyone in the room know that she'd be leaving with him, this woman who had no idea how beautiful she was.

Leonie was sure her heart was beating faster than it ever had before when they finally made it to the bedroom at Jacques' villa. The journey had seemed to take for ever although, when she glanced at the clock on the bedside table, it wasn't as late as she'd thought.

Part of her wanted to rewind, to go to that moment on the terrace when she'd told him she'd changed her mind, to take back the words.

But that part of her was a coward, and the part that wasn't a coward was scared to death.

Being in her forties was fine in theory. If she'd still been married, she wouldn't have had a problem with her age at all, but then she wouldn't have been here with a gorgeous man, planning to undress.

She just wasn't prepared for this.

She was a grown woman, a woman who'd had children; she wasn't some naïve girl. She knew what was involved, but she'd only ever had sex with *one man*. And this wasn't him.

She didn't know what she was supposed to do. There was no way she was going to calmly take off her clothes in front of him. Besides, her hands were shaking too much to deal with anything so

technical; just standing up was difficult enough
with her heart thumping so hard and fast.

Jacques came to her then, and, without giving
her time to have one more thought, kissed her so
deeply a wave of heat and long-suppressed sen-
sations swept over her nerve endings, leaving her
tingling and needy.

His mouth moved tantalisingly down her throat
and she dropped her head back, moaning for
more, but when his fingertips slipped beneath the
edge of her dress and slid under her bra strap, she
jerked away.

'Wait!'

His hands dropped to his sides and he watched
solemnly as she went to the lamp and switched it
off. She straightened, realising then that the
moonlight pouring through the open window had
made the lamp superfluous anyway. With a small
sigh she crossed to the window and reached for a
shutter, but Jacques' hand stopped hers.

He was right behind her. 'Don't be scared,' he
said as he tugged her gently back into the room.

'I'm not *scared*.'

She'd never been a good actress and she knew
she was fooling no one.

'Yes, you are.' He pulled her into his arms and
held her. 'It's been a long time for you, hasn't it?'

She sank against him. He felt so solid and

secure that she relaxed again. 'There's never been anyone but my husband,' she whispered.

His hold tightened, and he nodded. After a pause, he went on. 'We can take this slowly. As slowly as you like. We can just sleep together if that's what you want. But…' His lips brushed her ear. 'Don't hide from me. Let me see you.'

She shuddered, but in a good way. The tingling of his voice against her ear rippled all the way down her limbs. She leaned back so that she could see his face. In the moonlight, he looked like the man from her dreams. And she wanted him. She wanted what he'd given her in those dreams and she was not going to back out now.

Satisfied. Satiated. And smug.

That was how she felt when she stretched out in the recliner on the balcony outside Jacques' bedroom. She snuggled further into the towelling robe he'd lent her after their shower, and sighed. Thinking back, she had no idea what she'd been afraid of. She should have known that making love with Jacques would be wonderful. Beyond wonderful. He took his time over each and every aspect of it.

He'd gone out to get some breakfast, and she thought about taking the opportunity to ring Samantha, but then decided against it. Sam would be sure to hear something in her voice that would make her ask questions, and Leonie did not want to lie to Sam, but she didn't want to share this new development with her either.

Hearing a door bang and footsteps on the stairs, she twisted in her seat, eager to catch the first glimpse of him. She was rewarded with the heart-stopping sight of Jacques in jeans that sat low on his hips and a T-shirt that hugged his upper body.

He might not be a young man, but he was fit and toned. She could vouch for it after sharing his bed. She'd loved the feel of his hard muscles under her hands.

He smiled when he saw her and, after placing his purchases on the wrought-iron table, came around to kiss her. She put her hands on either side of his face, finding his cheeks rough because he hadn't shaved yet. 'You were gone so long.'

Laughing, he took hold of her hands, kissed both palms, then straightened. 'I was extra quick. The croissants are still hot.'

'Ooh.' She sat up at the mention of food. It wouldn't matter what he'd brought, she was so hungry she'd eat anything. She hadn't realised that sex could be such good exercise. Or so passionate, or so…fulfilling.

Jacques disappeared downstairs to fetch glasses

for the fresh orange juice he'd brought back, and, too hungry to wait, she started to eat without him.

Despite her warnings to herself, she knew she'd already become way too attached to him to walk away without a backward glance. Leaving was going to be tough; she wouldn't kid herself it could be any other way. But she'd handle that when the time came, and she wouldn't worry about it now. For now, everything was perfect. She felt alive again.

He returned with the glasses and while she poured the juice into them, he asked, 'What would you like to do today?'

'Mmm, that's a good question.' She stopped pouring and looked up, her face straight. 'I know what I'd *like* to do, but I don't know whether you'd be up to it. Not *all* day anyway. You are older than me, after all.' She broke into a grin.

He laughed, his eyes gleaming. 'I think we can safely assume that you are over your shyness.'

'Oh, yes, you fixed that, all right.' He had cured it by making her feel beautiful. He'd left her in no doubt that she was desirable. And it felt good.

Still laughing, he said, 'I do have a suggestion. What about a trip to Monte Carlo? It won't take long to drive there and you should probably see it if this is your one and only visit to the Riviera. We could stay overnight.'

Her eyes widened. 'Oh, wow, that sounds good. But don't you have to work? And what about Antoine?'

'I do normally spend Mondays with Antoine, but this week I've arranged to take a couple of days off work, and it will only mean one night away from home so Antoine won't have chance to miss me. You should see the Monte Carlo night-life, visit the casino.'

'I'm not a gambler. I wouldn't have a clue what to do in a casino.'

'That's all right, I'm not a gambler either. We could just walk around and watch the experts play, if you like. At least you'll be able to tell your children that you've been to the Monte Carlo casino.'

She chuckled. 'They won't believe it. I'll have to take a photo on my phone and send it to them.' They wouldn't believe it if they knew who she was staying overnight with either. Actually, they'd find that much more difficult to believe and even harder to accept.

She wouldn't do that to them, of course. No way. They'd lost their father; they did not deserve to lose their mother as they knew her. She would go back to being that woman when she went home, and they would never need to know that she'd had a brief, passionate fling with a handsome Frenchman.

Her throat tightened, causing her to choke on the mouthful of croissant she attempted to swallow. It was a reaction, she knew, to the idea of leaving all this behind. But lots of women had holiday romances, and got over them easily enough. And that was all this could be. She mustn't start thinking of it as anything more.

They stopped at the village of La Turbie to see the Roman ruins of Le Trophée des Alpes, and from the terraces of the monument the spectacular panorama taking in Monaco seemed breathtakingly close.

Despite the delay, they arrived in Monaco in time to see the changing of the guard, which Leonie loved, then they did a tour of the palace, and even entered the church where Princess Grace had been married and buried.

After lunch, they took the little tourist train around the highlights of the principality. Sitting so close to Jacques that their thighs were pressed together, Leonie leaned her head on his shoulder. The breeze blew her hair across her face and Jacques tenderly stroked it aside, then hugged her to his side.

'No regrets?'

'About last night? Yes,' she said with a dramatic sigh.

His eyes narrowed. 'Do you mean it?'

'I regret that I waited so long.'

After searching her face, he broke into a smile. 'That's all you regret?'

'Well, that and the fact that you couldn't keep up with me.'

He laughed so loudly that other passengers turned to look at them.

She shushed him, then said in a lower voice, 'No, not really. Neither of us did badly for our age.'

Jacques made an exasperated gesture.

The French had gestures to express almost every sentiment, she thought, then she smiled. 'I know, I know. We're not old.' And she didn't feel it either. She was still buzzing with the discoveries she'd made about her own body. Maybe later, she'd come crashing down and remember her age, but for now she was going to enjoy this while she could.

After getting off the train, they drove on into Monte Carlo, where every car they saw on the road was a Ferrari, a Porsche, or something equally upmarket, and checked into their suite. Enormous and luxurious, it would have been a great location for a honeymoon, she thought, and before she could stop them memories of her honeymoon with Shane popped into her head.

It hadn't been much of one. They hadn't been able to afford a hotel. A couple of nights in a caravan had been all they'd been able to stretch to. It hadn't been romantic, but they'd enjoyed it. Although now that she thought of it, they hadn't spent much time in bed—it was the location that they'd enjoyed most. They had loved each other dearly, just not in a passionate way.

And that was when she realised that she'd been able to think about Shane without getting all teary-eyed and sad. He'd been a huge part of her life, of course, but her life hadn't ended when his had, and it seemed she really was ready to move on. Maybe she had Jacques to thank for that, or maybe it would have happened regardless. Either way, she couldn't help being glad that she'd met Jacques and that he'd shown her what lovemaking could be. Not that she would have missed it if she'd never known, but…well, she was just very, very glad.

The days flew by. She still attended classes most days, and Jacques still worked at the restaurant, where she would often join him and sit at the bar watching him do his thing. Every other moment, they spent together, just the two of them. Sometimes out and about, but more often at Jacques' villa where they talked and laughed together, and, frequently, they spent the night there too.

One Sunday morning, she woke with Jacques' arm curled around her waist possessively. If he thought she was likely to attempt an escape, he was wrong. She didn't want to be anywhere but with him. With his chest moving rhythmically against her back as he breathed, she was at peace. More than that, she couldn't remember the last time she'd been so happy.

Did she deserve all this?

If she'd ever imagined finding a new man, she would have pictured herself becoming friendly with a fellow member of one of the clubs she'd planned to join. Gardening, perhaps. Or pottery. T'ai chi was the most adventurous she'd envisaged. And their shared interest would have led to cups of tea and companionship.

Never could she have seen herself as the type to meet—better yet, proposition—a man who ran one of the Riviera's most highly rated restaurants.

Of course, she hadn't exactly propositioned Jacques, but she had been the one to make the first move. He would have kept his promise if she hadn't told him bluntly that she didn't want him to do so.

Her stomach shook with silent laughter as she remembered her trepidation. It was hard to imagine now, here in Jacques' arms, that she hadn't thrown herself at him at the first opportunity.

Her slight movement must have disturbed him because his breathing changed and then he nuzzled the nape of her neck.

'Mmm-mmm.' She rolled onto her back, his

heavy arm still pinning her to the bed. 'Good morning.'

'Yes, it is. You're here.'

'Oh, that's sweet.' She kissed him. 'We'd better get moving or you'll be late.'

He lifted his head to look at the clock on the bedside table, then groaned. 'How did that happen? How did it get to be so late?'

She laughed. 'We must be too old to spend half the night—'

'No.' He hugged her closer. 'We're in the prime of our lives.'

'You've made me feel like that's true.'

'It *is* true.'

'You're good for me, Jacques.' She sighed. 'I'm so glad I met you.'

'So am I.' Very tenderly, he kissed her on the lips.

She sighed again. 'I'd better jump in the shower before we get sidetracked.'

'I'll make breakfast.'

When, eventually, she emerged from the bathroom, he'd eaten breakfast and hers was laid out on the balcony table. The doors were open and the warm autumn sunshine filled the room as she wrapped the robe around her, then made her way outside.

He looked across and smiled. 'You look so sexy with your hair wet and scraped back like that.'

'Really?' She picked up a just-warm croissant. 'Well, hold that thought. There's always
this afternoon.'

'Ah, no. Not this afternoon. I have to drive
home, remember. I spend Mondays with Antoine.
I won't see you till Tuesday.'

Disappointment dowsed her good mood. She'd
forgotten. She should be used to it since he stayed
at home every Monday, and she didn't begrudge his
son this regular time with his father, not one little
bit, but after they'd had such a wonderful night she
hated the thought of not seeing him till Tuesday.

She brightened. 'I know,' she said with a grin,
'I'll come with you. It will be great. I'd love to
meet Antoine, to see where you grew up, and—'

'No.' He was shaking his head and she couldn't
understand why.

'No?' She wrinkled her nose at him. 'No, what?'

He shook his head.

'That's all you're going to say? No?'

He sighed and pushed a hand through his hair.
'Look…I don't do that.'

'What don't you do?'

Shooting her a pained look, he said, 'I don't
take women to the vineyard.'

The jolt hit her as if she'd been punched in the
stomach. Hard and fast and breathtaking.

'I'm sorry, it's just that I prefer to keep any

affairs I have here separate from my life at home with my family. I thought you understood. I don't like to mix the two. They have nothing to do with each other.'

She should have known—she did know—that she wasn't special to him. How could she be? She was just an ageing tourist who'd caught his eye and provided some light entertainment. She wasn't the sort of woman he'd introduce to his family.

Swallowing hard, she managed to say, 'I see.'

He studied her face for a moment, but she kept it rigid, refusing to let him see how she felt.

'Do you?'

She nodded. There was an ache at the back of her throat that would have made it too difficult to speak at that moment.

Getting to his feet, he said, 'Well, I'll have a shower. Enjoy your breakfast.'

She nodded again, turning her face away.

As soon as the bathroom door had closed, she took a deep breath, then dropped the uneaten portion of the croissant to her plate. She brushed the crumbs from her hands, left the table and found her clothes. Having dressed quickly, she grabbed her bag and had left the house before Jacques had even finished his shower.

If she walked fast it would only take her half an hour to reach her apartment, and a fast walk was just what she needed to take away the sting of what had happened back there.

Was it really less than an hour since she'd woken in his arms and everything had seemed wonderful?

CHAPTER EIGHT

'I DON'T understand the problem,' Chantal said after several clicks of her tongue. 'You are having a good time with him, no?'

'I was.' Leonie got out of the chair and crossed to the open window. 'Oh, I knew it wasn't going to last. I was prepared for that. I knew it was never going to be a proper relationship and that was part of the attraction of it, but, still, I thought I meant more to him than just another—' She bit off the word she'd been about to say. It wasn't like her to use such language. She must be angrier than she thought. 'Just another of his women,' she said instead.

Chantal threw up her hands. 'You say the word as if it is something bad. What is wrong with being a woman? It's not as if he called you a mistress.'

A chill stiffened her spine and spread through her bones. Gasping, Leonie turned. 'I hadn't thought…maybe that's why he doesn't want me to go with him. Maybe he has a wife.'

'*Ah, mais, non.* I did not mean that.' Chantal gave her a sharp look. 'You don't think so, do you?'

Well, did she?

She turned back to the window and considered the question, considered the Jacques she'd come to know, and she'd have said she knew him pretty well until this had happened. But even now she couldn't reconcile the cheating-husband image with the Jacques she knew. And even in this incident he'd been honest with her. She just didn't like the truth.

She shook her head. 'No. He's not the sort of man who would do that. He told me he was single.'

'So...' Chantal shrugged. 'You have nothing to worry about, do you? You're just annoyed because you had to stay here without him.'

Leonie frowned. Chantal saw the situation quite differently from her. Was that a cultural thing, or did it mean she'd overreacted? It wasn't as if she were an expert in male-female relationships.

'I guess I'll just have to face the fact that he doesn't want me to meet his family because I'm no more important to him than any of the other women he's had brief flings with. He's just not serious about me.'

'Which is what you knew all along. And you're

not serious about him either,' Chantal pointed out helpfully, but Leonie winced.

If she wasn't serious about him, why had this whole incident hurt so deeply?

She plonked herself down in the armchair and sighed. No, she wasn't supposed to be serious. This was meant to be a harmless holiday romance, a no-strings, short-term affair, but she'd slipped up badly. She'd allowed him to burrow deep under her skin, right through her flesh and into her heart.

Quite simply, she'd fallen in love.

And that explained a lot. Like the need to see him every day, the jolt to her heart each time she did see him however short the separation, and the sensation of falling whenever he kissed her. She really had been falling. For him.

It took a moment for the reality of this admission to sink in. The reality she hadn't wanted to see despite all the evidence.

But she couldn't be blamed for not believing it could happen. If anyone had asked her when she first arrived in France whether there was even the slightest chance of her falling in love, she'd have laughed. Against all probability she'd not only found a man she *could* fall in love with, but she'd had the bad sense to do exactly that.

He, on the other hand, had been infinitely more sensible. He hadn't let her become too important to him. He'd stuck to their bargain. He'd shown her how to have fun. He'd shown her a lot more than that too.

She remembered his tender kisses of the previous day. He cared about her, that much was obvious, but she'd known he liked her before they'd slept together. She wouldn't have taken that massive step otherwise.

He would find it much easier to say goodbye than her, and she envied him that. Not that she wanted him to suffer the way she would, nor would she let him know that she was suffering.

She wouldn't tell him that she loved him, wouldn't reveal how silly she'd been. He'd gone into this relationship believing she was mature enough to control her emotions. It would be better for both of them if she kept her feelings to herself.

She sighed. None of it was his fault. She'd known exactly what she was getting into—and it wasn't as if there were any chance of staying permanently, even if he had wanted her to. She had responsibilities back home. Her life was there. Her family was there. Her future was there.

'He hasn't done anything wrong.'

Chantal nodded. 'I agree.'

Leonie wondered whether things would be the same when Jacques returned from the vineyard, or whether he'd decide she was taking things too seriously. She wouldn't blame him if he did.

But she'd have plenty of years without him once she went home. She didn't want their affair to end here and now. Not when they still had a few weeks left. She'd have to tell him that she understood why, and accepted that he didn't want to introduce her to his family.

It wouldn't hurt her to go to school the next day. It was about time she made an appearance again. In the meantime, she had a Sunday afternoon to fill. She looked across at Chantal. 'Do you want to go out?'

Chantal shrugged. 'Where would we go? Remember, I am an old woman.'

'You're not old…' Leonie paused, remembering all the times she'd referred to herself as old, and Chantal was probably twenty years her senior. 'No, you're not old, but we'll just go for a short walk, and we'll call into a café that I go to often. It's not far from here.' Actually, she hadn't been there so often since she and Jacques had started sleeping together. They'd been too absorbed in each other to want to be around other people.

Jacques had driven halfway home before he let himself remember the look of disappointment on Leonie's face. When he'd returned to the bedroom to find her gone, he'd thought she was angry that he put Antoine first, that he'd chosen to go home over spending the next day and a half with her. And he'd been angry himself then, because she'd known from the beginning that Antoine meant the world to him. How could she possibly expect him to give up the one free day he had with his son in order to spend it with her?

Now, though, the anger had evaporated, and he'd realised something. He'd hurt her.

She wasn't jealous of Antoine. Better than anyone, she understood his love for his son. She was hurt by his refusal to take her to his home, to introduce her to his family. Even now he could see the change in her expression as his words had struck her. The words that had told her she was no more important than any of the other women he'd had casual relationships with. Not that there had been many, but she knew there had been a few.

How could he have been so insensitive?

She meant more to him than those other women. Of course she did. There was no comparison between the short-term search for mutual satisfaction he'd shared with each of them, and what he had with Leonie.

After a slow stroll around the old town during which Chantal pointed out places of interest from her past, Leonie stopped outside Jean-Claude's café.

'Ah, yes, I remember this place. It used to be run by friends of ours, Jean-Claude and Renée.'

'Well, Jean-Claude is still here. I've never met Renée, though. I'm pretty sure Jean-Claude is on his own now.'

'Ah.' Chantal looked sad for a moment, then she nodded and headed for the door.

Jean-Claude came to serve them and Leonie couldn't help smiling at his classic double take.

'Chantal? It is you?'

Within moments, the two old friends were chatting, and Leonie heard Jean-Claude say that his wife had passed away. Sitting on one of the stools at the counter, she sipped her hot coffee, breathing in the rich aroma that never failed to thrill her.

The door opened, allowing sunshine to spill inside, and she turned towards it, but at first she could see nothing against the glare. Then the door closed, her eyes adjusted, and she found herself looking straight into a familiar pair of warm brown eyes.

'Jacques!' Her heart leapt at the sight of him. She slipped off the stool, drawn towards him without thinking. 'What…what are you doing here?'

'Looking for you.'

'But you're supposed to be at the vineyard. Is there something wrong?'

Lips pressed together, he nodded. 'I didn't make it there. I came back to talk to you. Can we sit down?'

He still hadn't smiled, and when he jerked his head towards an empty table, she said, 'I'll just let Chantal know.'

He looked at the older woman in surprise. 'Your neighbour?'

'We came out for a walk and stopped off here for a coffee. It turns out that she knows Jean-Claude from way back.'

His eyebrows rose as he looked at his old friend, who was far more animated than Leonie had ever seen him.

'It could be good for both of them,' she said. 'Chatting about old times.'

'Yes.' After a moment, he turned away to squeeze between the tables while she went to Chantal and touched her on the forearm.

'I'll be over there for a minute or two.' She pointed in the direction of Jacques' table.

'Ah.' Chantal nodded. 'He doesn't look very happy.'

'No.' She bit her lip before fetching her coffee from the counter and carrying it over to the table. 'Do you want a coffee?'

He shook his head, and she sat down. 'So, won't Antoine be disappointed?'

'I spoke to him on the phone. He knows I'll be late.' He paused, giving her a serious look. 'You left the villa while I was in the shower.'

She dipped her head. 'I shouldn't have done that. I'm sorry.'

Frowning, he said, 'No, don't apologise. That's what I came here to do. I have reason to apologise, don't I?'

'No.' Her voice was low and she stared into her coffee, but then she looked up, determined to show him that she was capable of having an adult relationship. 'I do see your point. You wouldn't want your family to meet every woman you have a brief affair with. They'd get tired of an endless procession of women.'

He winced, then murmured something unintelligible. 'There have not been many women at all. It would certainly not be an endless procession.' He made a frustrated gesture. 'But that is not the point. I wouldn't have wanted them to meet any of the others. I *do* want them to meet you.'

He reached for her hand and she turned it palm-up so he could clasp it. It felt so good to be touching him again. She couldn't believe she'd nearly thrown away the chance just because she'd taken offence, and all over nothing. He ran his thumb over her knuckles, and her stomach clenched with need for him.

'I am sorry that I hurt you by implying that you were not different.'

She looked up from their joined hands, not bothering to deny it, thankful that he understood her well enough to have worked it out.

'I would like to show you the vineyard, and the house and the village. I think you'd enjoy seeing it all, and I know I would enjoy showing you. But I am worried about Antoine.'

'What? You don't think he'd like me?'

He surprised her by laughing. 'Quite the opposite. Of course he'll like you. He'll be completely entranced by you, just as I was.'

'Hey, wait a minute. Didn't you say once that he'd inherited your *poor* taste? What does that say about me?'

Her mock outrage made him laugh again. 'He has inherited a great deal from me, including both my good taste and my poor taste.'

She narrowed her eyes. 'Hmm, nice save. Well, anyway, I don't see the problem. I won't do anything to upset him.'

'No, I know you won't. But don't you see? Antoine will be devastated when you leave. It will be like Hélène all over again.' He shook his head, grimacing as he imagined the aftermath.

'Oh.' She allowed herself to dwell for just a moment on the fact that *he* wouldn't be devastated, then gave herself a mental shake.

'Well, if we make sure from the moment we meet that he understands I'm only on a visit, and stress the temporary nature of my stay here, he'll accept it at face value, won't he?'

Jacques looked thoughtful. 'Perhaps.'

She gave him a moment, then tilted her head. 'Surely he won't expect us to get married if we make it clear from the beginning that there's no chance of that?'

He gave her a small smile. 'How long will it take you to pack a bag?'

'Not long at all.'

'Then let's go.' As they got up from the table, he said, 'I'll bring you back on Tuesday morning, but next week is the festival of the *vendange*, celebrating the end of the grape harvest. Will you come home with me next week and stay for a few days?'

'I'd love to.'

He looked pleased. 'I was worried that I'd hurt you too much, that you wouldn't want to see me again.'

She nodded. 'I was a little worried myself— that you might think I was more trouble than I was worth.'

He lifted her hand and brushed his lips across her fingers. 'Never.'

'I'm glad you came back.'

'So am I.'

'We'll have to walk Chantal home first, by the way.'

But Chantal didn't want to leave.

'I will escort her home when I close up here,' Jean-Claude said. 'We are old friends. She knows she can trust me.'

'But you don't close till late.' Leonie looked from him to Chantal. 'You don't want to stay out that long, do you?'

Chantal looked unsure for a moment, then said, 'Why not? At my age I don't sleep so well. I might as well stay here. Besides, I am having fun.'

Sitting next to Jacques as they drove through vine-yards and orchards, Leonie knew already that she was going to love this place that was his home. Vines she had expected, but not the silver-leafed olives, nor the pine forests and wildflowers.

The Arrière-Pays was about the furthest thing imaginable from the fast pace of Nice. It was different from anything she'd seen before, but also reminded her of her own home in places where the grass had turned golden after a long, dry summer.

Jacques pointed out a roadside sign, and sudden apprehension gripped her. It hadn't occurred to her before, but what if his family didn't like her? She could be stuck here with people who hated her, this foreigner who'd intruded on their family time.

He turned into the long driveway to the vineyard. Tall pine trees stood on either side of the driveway, like soldiers standing to attention in a guard of honour. Her stomach bubbled with anxiety. She should have spent some time asking Jacques about his family, their likes and dislikes, preparing herself to meet them. Instead, she was coming in cold, with no idea how to make them like her.

It was too late now to do anything but hope for the best, so she drew in a deep breath. If they were anything like Jacques, they'd be nice people.

'I forgot to ask, do they speak English?'

He smiled across at her. 'Yes, they all do, even Antoine, but you wouldn't need to worry anyway. You speak French well enough now.'

'You think so?' Her spirits lifted. 'I have learned a lot. More than I thought I would when I first started.'

He nodded. 'Yes, you've done well.' Pointing, he said, 'There's the house.'

The driveway opened to a large stony area

behind which stood the house, glowing silver in the afternoon sun. Large and solid, like the chalky hills in the background, it had periwinkle-blue shutters and a faded terracotta roof.

It took her breath away.

'It's beautiful,' she said when she got her breath back.

Jacques smiled, then drove the car around the side of the house, parking it in the shade of an enormous tree that must have been very, very old.

She got out of the car. From here she could see more stone buildings at some distance from the house, and a modern building too. 'Are those buildings on your family's land?'

'That's the winery,' he said. 'We'll look around there tomorrow. Bertrand will want to be with us.' He took her bag from the car. 'I should have said, my mother will probably put you in a separate room. It might be better…if Antoine doesn't see us going into the same room.'

'Oh, absolutely, I understand.' She squeezed his hand. 'Your family doesn't need to know that we've been sleeping together. Goodness, I wouldn't want my children to know either. There's no need to advertise the fact.'

She dropped his hand then. 'Oops.' She gave a rueful shrug. 'Nearly gave the game away already.'

He laughed, but shook his head. 'I'm going to

miss you tonight.' He brushed one finger down her cheek. 'Think about me before you go to sleep,' he said, then led her into the house.

As if she'd have any choice but to think about him. She followed, and his mother came to greet her just inside the door. A slim, well-groomed woman, she was polite, but her face had a stern look. Leonie didn't feel particularly welcome, but decided that all she could do was be herself. If his mother still didn't like her, that was just the way it had to be.

So, she smiled and asked questions in her usual forthright way, questions about the house and the family photographs on the wall, and slowly Madame Broussard softened a little.

They chatted until Jacques told his mother he wanted to introduce Leonie to Antoine. The three of them headed for the back of the house where the boy was sitting in the shade of a vine-covered courtyard, playing on a hand-held game console.

He looked up and grinned. *'Papa!'*

Leonie watched Jacques crouch beside the wheelchair and draw the boy into a hug that melted her insides. If she hadn't already fallen in love with him, she would have done so in that moment.

Jacques straightened, and pointed out that they had a visitor. Leonie stepped forward, smiling.

'Bonjour,' Antoine said in a bright voice.

'*Bonjour* to you too.' She turned a chair from the table and moved it so that she could sit next to him. 'My son used to have one of these.' She pointed to the game console in his lap. 'In fact, he had that game.'

'How old is he?'

'Eighteen. He's at university now. I used to be pretty good at it too. We spent a bit of time at the hospital waiting for his father, so we used to challenge each other.'

'Do you want a go?' He held it out and she smiled as she took it from him.

'Thanks. What's your score?'

A short time later, Leonie was aware of Jacques and his mother going back inside the house, but she didn't look up. She felt it was important to let Antoine see she was telling the truth about being good at the game, not just making empty conversation.

In the kitchen, Jacques took the tray from his mother and moved towards the back door.

'She's different, this one.'

'What?' He looked over his shoulder at his mother.

'This Leonie. She's different from the last woman you brought here—that Hélène.'

'Oh, yes, she's definitely different from Hélène,

but it's a different situation, Mother. Hélène was my fiancée. Leonie and I are not serious.'

'Not serious, hmm?'

'No, and I don't want Antoine to get the idea that we are.'

He carried the tray outside, stopping in his tracks when he saw Leonie and Antoine laughing together. She looked beautiful, her eyes shining as she grinned at his son. And she looked so *right* there.

Leonie turned and saw them. Even his mother's severe expression softened further under the force of her beaming smile.

'I'm hopeless,' she said. 'I thought I'd do okay. I used to be quite good, but Antoine is way, way better than me.'

'The ability to use one of those things is inversely proportionate to age, isn't it?' he said as he set the tray on the old table. 'The greater the years, the lower the score.'

'Oh, thanks.' She laughed again. 'That makes me ancient.'

'Well, leave that now,' his mother said, flapping her hand at them. 'Sit at the table. Bertrand said he would join us for coffee— Ah, here he is.'

Jacques greeted his brother, then introduced Leonie. Bertrand's eyes lit up with curiosity and he immediately claimed the chair next to hers. As

Antoine's wheelchair was on her other side, Jacques had no choice but to sit across the table. Still, it gave him the opportunity to watch her, and he had to make the most of that since he wouldn't be able to hold her for a couple of days.

'So, you're coming back next week for the festival?' his brother asked.

Leonie nodded. 'Jacques said it would be a good time to visit.'

'We'll do our best to make sure you enjoy it. Many people say the region is at its best at this time of year. You should take the opportunity to look around.'

'Oh, well, I will if possible. What I've seen so far looks beautiful.'

'Personally,' Bertrand said, 'I like spring best, when all the vines are bursting into growth and there's so much promise for the year's harvest.'

She nodded.

'I like winter,' Antoine said. 'When the vines are cut back into little stumps.'

'And the wind blows,' Jacques added. He looked at Leonie. 'Not many people like winter, but Antoine and I do. The Mistral…it blows so hard it knocks over trees and damages houses and makes everyone irritable.'

'It rains,' Madame Broussard said, passing out cups of coffee. 'And it's cold.'

'But the wind dries the moisture in the sky, leaving it a deep blue colour,' Jacques went on. 'It dries the vines, and purifies the vineyard.'

Antoine tapped Leonie's arm to get her attention and she was smiling as she turned to him. 'Will you come back to visit us in winter? Then you'll see why we like it.'

'Oh.'

Jacques saw her face fall for a moment, but she recovered quickly.

'I'm afraid I can't. I'll be home by then. In Australia.'

'You could come back, couldn't you? You could fly.'

Bertrand laughed. 'It's too far, Antoine. It takes a whole day and night to fly there.'

'But—'

'Antoine, that's enough,' Jacques said, firmly but gently. He had the uncomfortable feeling that his son was already under Leonie's spell and she'd only been there—what?—less than an hour?

Perhaps this visit had not been one of his better ideas. He didn't let people inside his life like this for a reason—and here it was.

'People like to visit different places when they go on holiday,' he said to his son now. 'Not the same place over and over again.'

But some people did revisit locations where

they'd had a good time. He wondered whether Leonie had enjoyed herself enough that she would want to come back one day. Would she decide to drop in on her way to some other destination? Or would this visit be all they would ever have?

'So, you have family?' his mother asked her, saving him from having to continue, and he was glad of it. 'You said you had a son…?'

'Yes.' Leonie's voice cracked a little as if she too had been deep in less-than-happy thought. He looked up, but she cleared her throat and smiled that sunny smile he'd come to know so well. 'I have two wonderful children,' she said proudly.

While she went on to tell his mother and brother all about her family, and about her home in Australia, he looked across at Antoine. The boy was listening to every word. Jacques' heart sank. He was right. Antoine was hooked, and he should have known it would happen. Hadn't he himself been captivated by her charm the first time he'd met her? And his son wasn't like other children. He was not so resilient.

He'd made a mistake bringing her here. It was going to happen again. Antoine was going to be hurt. This time, though, Antoine wouldn't be the only one.

He should have been hurt by Hélène deserting him, but all he'd felt was anger and bitterness. It would be very different with Leonie. His chest tightened as he thought about watching her leave. If he thought there was any hope…

But no, there was no chance of her staying, she'd made that very clear. And he wouldn't ask her to.

His jaw taut, he looked down at his fists where they were pressing into his thighs. He looked up a moment later into his brother's narrowed eyes. Giving himself a mental shake, he made an effort to join in the conversation.

Leonie was alone in the kitchen with Jacques' mother later when the older lady suddenly sat down with a groan.

'What is it?' she asked in alarm, crossing the room to her side.

'It's nothing.' Madame Broussard waved her hand. 'It's just my back. It protests sometimes that I'm getting old and shouldn't be doing all the lifting that I do.'

Leonie frowned. 'It's right. I mean, not about you getting old, of course.' She sat in the next chair. 'By lifting, do you mean looking after Antoine?'

She nodded. 'Jacques does as much as he can, and Bertrand helps when Jacques is at work.'

'But it's still too much.'

She twisted the lace tablecloth, then seemed to

see what she was doing and smoothed it out again. 'It's a pity he doesn't have a wife.'

'Yes.' Leonie hesitated. 'But I don't think he wants one.'

'No.' She grimaced. 'He's had bad luck with women.'

'I know. He's told me.'

His mother looked at her in surprise. 'Has he? About his first wife?'

She nodded.

'But he never talks about it.' Then she shrugged. 'Of course, I don't know what he does in Nice. He might tell a lot of people.'

'No, I don't think so.' Leonie moistened her lips. 'He told me about the other woman as well, the one he was going to marry a few years ago.'

'Yes. That one.' Her eyes rolled. 'Nasty woman.'

Leonie nodded, even though she'd never met the woman. It was enough to know what she'd done. 'I'm sure she put him off trying again.'

His mother sighed. 'Yes, she did. But not all women are like her. There are some who like children, even special children like Antoine. There's you.'

Leonie bit her lip before saying, 'Yes, I love children, and I already like Antoine. But I have a family of my own.' She paused, feeling awkward, then went on, 'And I'm only here for a short time.'

His mother levered herself out of the chair. 'I know. As I said, he has bad luck with women. I must start to cook dinner.'

Leonie's offer of help was declined, so she went off to find Jacques, but with no intention of telling him about their conversation.

CHAPTER NINE

DINNER that night was…interesting. Jacques' mother had made beef *en croûte,* a dish that Leonie had eaten elsewhere, but Madame Broussard had packed a profusion of herbs between the meat and the crust, making it even more delicious than usual.

But it wasn't the meal that Leonie was thinking about when she went up to bed that night. It was Bertrand's behaviour. He was definitely flirting with her, and she wasn't the only one who'd got the message. Jacques had become more and more irritated with his brother, to the point where she'd expected a huge row to burst out, and she'd been preparing to mediate. But it hadn't, because Bertrand had suddenly backed off.

She shook her head, unsure how to take him. Did he really like her? Or was he baiting his brother out of habit? But that made no sense unless he'd worked out that Jacques would be angry.

She did like Bertrand. He was enough like Jacques to make it impossible not to, slightly taller, more grey hair, but the resemblance was strong. And then, he was also different. It was one of those indefinable things; she couldn't explain why, but she just didn't feel the slightest attraction to Bertrand.

Jacques, she remembered, had attracted her straightaway, even if she hadn't recognised or admitted it until much later.

The discussion during and after dinner had been lively with much arm waving and pursing of lips. Very much as she'd expected a French family to converse. Jacques had patiently explained the bits that she didn't catch.

Later, she unpacked her bag in the simply but tastefully furnished room she'd been given. Decorated in a white-on-white colour scheme, it was classy in an understated way. Which pretty much described the Broussards, she thought as she climbed into bed.

Bertrand escorted them to the winery the next day. 'You've come at a good time,' he said as he led them inside the first of the big stone sheds. 'The grapes have just been crushed so you can taste the juice.' He fetched her a tiny glass.

She took it from him and sipped it. 'I have no

idea what it's supposed to taste like, so I don't know whether it's good or bad.'

'There is no good or bad. There's too sweet, or too acidic. But that's where I come in. I blend the wine, adding or subtracting, until it's just right for the new vintage.'

'Bertrand thinks he's the only one who can blend a Domaine Broussard wine,' Jacques said. 'He's wrong, of course.'

'Ah, little brother, while I'm in charge here, no one else will blend a wine.'

'Even though someone else might do a better job.'

'Might. Might. Is it worth the risk?'

Leonie began to see why these two brothers couldn't work together. 'So what happens to the juice?' she asked, intervening as she had many times between Samantha and Kyle. Not that she thought there was anything remotely childlike about either of them, but she could see this discussion deteriorating at a rapid pace if she didn't step in.

Bertrand explained the process as he guided them through the sheds, showing them the machines and the steel vats. Leonie was genuinely interested. She'd never toured a winery before, and to know that this one dated back to the sixteenth century was mind-blowing.

Jacques' family had tended the grapes and

produced the wine throughout all of that time. Just the thought of the history made her a little dizzy, and that was before she entered the cool cellar and was hit by the intoxicating, almost overpowering aroma of wine.

'I opened a bottle this afternoon when I heard that you'd arrived.' Bertrand led her over to a stone table set against the arched stone wall and lifted a bottle, which he displayed proudly.

Leonie nodded. 'That was very kind of you.'

'Well, it's not often that such a beautiful woman visits our winery. It's an event worth celebrating.'

She laughed, then glanced at Jacques, who was looking a little wary as his brother poured three glasses of deep red wine.

'This was a great vintage,' Jacques said, taking a glass from the table.

'Yes, it was.'

'Tell us what you think,' Bertrand said as he handed her a glass.

She thanked him as she took it. 'I won't be able to do it justice, though. I'm such a novice.'

But when she tasted it, she was very impressed at the way it slid over her tongue. By the time she'd realised that Jacques and Bertrand had spit theirs out, she'd already swallowed hers. She shrugged when they both looked at her. 'It's too good to waste.'

'You're right.' Jacques swallowed a mouthful of his.

Bertrand laughed. 'Thank you for the compliment. I have to go out on some business, but stay and drink your wine. I probably won't see you again before you leave tomorrow morning, but I'll look forward to seeing you next week.' He gave her a slow smile and for a moment she wondered whether he was going to start flirting with her again.

Deciding not to notice, she smiled back. 'Thank you so much for the tour.'

She waited till he'd left the cellar, then turned to Jacques with a wicked look. 'Does this mean we're all on our own down here?'

He tilted his head as if listening for signs of life. 'I believe we are.'

'Then…' She closed the space between them, pulled his head down and kissed him on the lips.

He sighed as he took her glass from her and placed it on the table. Then he pulled her into his arms and kissed her deeply.

His lips were hot in contrast to the chilly air of the cellar, his tongue firm and thrilling. She found the taste of him much more intoxicating than the wine.

She pressed herself against him, revelling in the sensation of his cold hands on her warm skin.

They were both breathing hard when he tore his mouth away, still holding her tightly. He let out a frustrated sound. 'We'd better stop… Someone could come in.'

'Okay.' She nodded, then took a deep breath and stepped away. 'Right.' She grabbed her half-full wine glass and downed the remaining contents.

'Right,' she said again, straightening her T-shirt. 'I'm ready now.'

Jacques closed his eyes. 'I'm not sure this was a good idea.' He exhaled and opened his eyes. 'Bringing you here, I mean. It's going to be difficult to keep my hands off you for the rest of the day. And next week it will be even longer.'

She giggled. It felt so good to know that she had this effect on him. That she—a middle-aged mother of two—could get him so worked up. And, of course, the effect was mutual, but she didn't want to cut short her visit because of it.

She straightened her shoulders. 'What are we—a pair of hormone-driven teenagers with no self-control? *No.* We're mature adults. We can do this. Of course we can.'

He gathered the wine bottle and glasses. 'Is that what you and Shane were? Hormone-driven teenagers?'

She walked beside him towards the exit. After a

moment's thought, she said, 'No, strangely enough, we weren't. We were friends. And then we were a married couple. But in between, there was none of this—' she flapped a hand between them '—this…well, chemistry, I suppose it's called.'

'Really?' He looked surprised. 'But you're such a passionate woman.'

She laughed. 'I didn't know that I was. I had no idea about that part of me until you brought it out.'

He stopped. In the dim light of the cellar, his eyes looked black. He murmured words that she couldn't understand. Then he took a deep breath. He seemed about to say something, but just then one of the winery workers clattered into the cellar in his heavy boots. He called a greeting to which Jacques responded.

When he looked back at her, he had a rueful smile on his face. 'Lucky we stopped when we did,' he said softly.

She nodded, grimacing. 'Okay, that's it. No more kissing until we get back to Nice.'

'This was not a good idea,' he said, shaking his head. He looked like a morose little boy.

She laughed. 'Maybe not, but I'm glad I came.'

She was also glad to have the opportunity to observe Jacques with his son. When she went with him to collect Antoine from school later that day, their loving interaction would have been charming to anyone who witnessed it, but to her it was a special delight.

One thing bothered her, and it was that maybe, just maybe, Jacques had a tendency to be a little overprotective of his son.

The following weekend, on Leonie's next visit, she leaned out of the window of her room, craning her neck to see what appeared to be a fairy-tale castle built right on top of a hill. She hadn't seen it the week before, but then she hadn't opened the window. She couldn't wait to ask Jacques about it.

Her room was at the back of the house so it over-looked the neatly laid-out garden full of roses, and some lavender bushes, and, beyond that, rows of vines in every direction. She could see the winery too and her stomach lurched at the sudden memory of the kiss she'd shared with Jacques in the aromatic cellar. She'd never sniff wine again without recalling the almost overwhelming passion that had nearly led them to be very, very reckless.

And just then her partner in crime came into her line of vision, pushing Antoine's chair along one of the garden paths. Her heart kicked against her breastbone as she watched. Antoine would grow up to look just like his father; she could see this already. They were talking and they hadn't seen her. She waited for them to near the house, then she waved. Spotting her at the same time, they both waved back.

'Come down,' Jacques called. 'We're ready to go to the festival.'

'Okay, I'm coming.' She hurried to fasten her flat sandals, then grabbed a sweater, which she tied around her shoulders. The day was sunny, but, being September, it was not quite as warm as it had been in previous weeks, and she felt she might need the extra warmth.

Downstairs, she found the family piling into the van. With seats for all of them, and room for Antoine's wheelchair, it was very practical.

Bertrand was the driver and somehow she ended up sitting next to him. He grinned across at her. 'Sleep well?'

'Very well, thank you. Oh, I meant to ask.' She twisted in her seat to talk to Jacques, but found he was busy discussing something with his mother, so she turned back to Bertrand. 'From my window, I could see the most amazing castle. Like something out of a fairy tale, and right on top of a hill.'

'That's where we're going,' he said. 'That's the local village. It's called a *village perché,* a perched village, because of the way the buildings cling to the hillside. There are several of them in this region. There is generally a fortified church right at the top, which, as you say, gives it the appearance of a fairy-tale castle.' He gave a very Gallic shrug. 'Maybe those castles were based on French perched villages? It's possible, no?'

'I should think so.'

He started the engine and they set off, driving through the vines to the winding road that led up the hill. Leonie was careful not to talk to Bertrand until he spoke to her, not wanting to disturb his concentration on the road, which was obviously not designed for twenty-first-century vehicles.

He was right about the buildings clinging to the hillsides. They seemed to grow right out of the rocks, as if they were something organic rather than man-made structures.

'Everything about the villages was designed to repel attackers,' Bertrand said as they drove through the heavy ramparts and entered the huddle of cobbled streets. 'But now many of them are under siege again. From foreign tourists, this time.' He smirked.

'To hear you and Jacques talk, anyone would think you hated tourists,' she said. 'But you don't really, do you?'

'No, not really.' He grinned. 'Especially not when they are as beautiful as you.'

She rolled her eyes but she couldn't help smiling. 'I told Jacques that I wasn't a tourist when we first met. I don't think he would have talked to me otherwise.'

'Oh, I think you're wrong about that.'

She laughed, then held her breath when he aimed the van at a slim space. It seemed impossibly small, but, sure enough, he manoeuvred the van into place and parked. She climbed out and went around to the back where Jacques and his mother were in the process of setting Antoine's chair on the cobbled surface.

'Oh, goodness, these streets must be terrible for the wheelchair.'

'Yes, they are.' Jacques grimaced. 'Which is why we only manage short bursts, then we take refuge at the café.'

She nodded. 'Sounds good.' She was glad she'd worn flat sandals too.

Bertrand locked the back door of the van, then pocketed the key. He smiled at her. 'I have to go and talk to some people so I'll see you at lunch. Save me a seat next to you, hmm?'

Jacques straightened. 'What about Francine?'

'She'll be too busy for lunch,' he said in an offhand manner. 'Till lunchtime, then.'

Leonie watched him stride off. 'Who's Francine?'

'She runs the café. The two of them have been a couple for as long as I can remember. Everyone expects them to marry eventually.'

'Then why is he flirting with me?' she said softly so that Madame Broussard wouldn't hear.

Jacques' lips pressed into a thin line, then he exhaled. 'That, I don't know. But I'm going to find out.'

They visited several stalls that were set up on one side of the village square, taking it in turns, the three of them, to push the wheelchair, and Antoine bumped over the cobbles between some of the stalls without their help. They tasted wine and other local produce, and Leonie bought a pretty fabric bag full of dried lavender. The fabric, Jacques' mother told her, was a traditional Provençal print dating back centuries. As she held it to her nose she thought about hanging it in her bedroom at home. Every time she went near it, the smell would remind her of Jacques.

Ha! As if she would ever forget him, lavender or no lavender. She dropped it into her bag and went back to the stall to buy lavender-scented bubble bath and soap.

Next, they headed for the sprawling outdoor café on the other side of the square. It was busy, but they found a table, and Leonie sat with Antoine and Jacques, while Madame Broussard went inside to see Francine. The sun was warm enough on her face to feel good, and she leaned back in her chair, relaxed and happy, surrounded by the hum of numerous conversations.

She rolled her head towards Antoine. 'So, apart from games, what do you like to do?' she asked.

He thought for a moment. 'I like cars.'

'Cars? What, models?'

'No.' He laughed as if she'd said something really stupid. 'Real cars. I can't wait till I'm old enough to drive. My dad says he'll buy me one of those cars with the hand controls.'

'Oh, right. That sounds good.' She shaded her eyes as she looked into his face. 'But that's later… What about now? Do you do any sport?'

'Sport?' He shook his head, looking puzzled.

'Wheelchair sports, I mean. Like basketball, rugby and so on. I wondered because the way you got yourself over those cobbles, you must have strong arms.'

He looked pleased. 'Yes, they are strong. But no, I don't do any sport.'

Jacques gave her a discouraging look.

Leonie raised her eyebrows. 'What?'

He sighed. 'That's enough talk of sports. Rugby is dangerous. People get hurt.'

'Well, basketball—'

'No.' He shook his head.

Leonie bit her tongue. Out of respect for Jacques' relationship with his son, she wouldn't argue in front of Antoine, but she made a mental note to bring it up with Jacques later, when they were alone. She knew that wheelchair sports were big back home. Of course, that was Australia where sport of all kinds was a large part of the fabric of life. There was a chance that a wheelchair team might be more difficult to find here, but it wouldn't be impossible, surely?

'Ah, here is Francine.'

Her head swivelled to see a lovely young woman heading their way, followed by Jacques' mother. As she neared the table Leonie could see that she wasn't as young as she'd seemed at first, but she was definitely lovely with her chin-length bob of black hair, huge dark eyes and cheekbones that would make a supermodel envious.

In her short black skirt and figure-hugging, short-sleeved sweater, she had that chic look that was purely French. They were all so well groomed, these women. Did they master grooming skills at the time they learned to walk? Because they certainly made her feel scruffy, even when she'd made an effort. It was undoubtedly a cultural thing, and, if she lived here, she wasn't sure she'd ever be able to fit in.

But what was she thinking? She would never

live here, so the problem of fitting in would never arise.

'*Bonjour, bonjour.*' Francine was greeting all of them with one of those melodic voices that made the French language sound like music. Far removed from her own butchered version of it, Leonie thought with a silent sigh.

She rose to be introduced to Francine and wondered what Bertrand was doing flirting with her if the lovely Francine was his girlfriend. She'd been right earlier; it made no sense at all.

Francine sat with them, and chatted while they drank their coffee. Eventually, though, she had to go back to work, but she promised that she was planning a delicious lunch for them.

They got to their feet, intending to move on to another part of the festival, but then Jacques' mother changed her mind. 'I think I'll just sit here and rest while you enjoy yourselves. Maybe I'll go inside. I can talk to Francine while she's working.'

She did look weary and Leonie was quite concerned about her. She didn't want to leave her but she insisted, and Jacques nodded.

'Francine will look after her,' he said to Leonie. 'And she's not ill, only tired.'

Leonie was still thinking about her while they gazed at a collection of terracotta *santons*, gaily painted traditional figures. The character-filled faces made her smile, but while Antoine was occupied with them she turned to Jacques and said in a low voice, 'Why don't you give your mother a break? She's tired and her back aches. Next week, why don't you take Antoine to your villa for the weekend?'

'I don't know.'

'What's not to know?'

He was thoughtful for a moment. 'It's not that simple. It requires two people to look after him properly, especially now that he's so big. When he was younger, it was easier.'

'But there will be two of us. I'll be there.'

At his frown, she wondered whether she'd been too presumptuous, but she dismissed the thought. There was nothing wrong with her suggestion. 'I know how to look after children, believe me.'

'I do believe you. I know you've had children, but Antoine is different.'

'No, he's not. He's a normal boy who can't walk.' She shook her head. 'I'm not trying to make light of the problems he faces, but there's no reason why he shouldn't come and spend a few days in Nice with us. We can manage, I promise.'

He didn't agree right away, but she knew he had come around to the idea when he asked Bertrand at lunch if he could swap vehicles with him for the coming weekend.

Bertrand agreed, and Leonie smiled.

CHAPTER TEN

JACQUES found his brother that night alone in his office at the front of the house. From the doorway he glanced around the room that had been their father's. Bertrand hadn't changed a thing.

Shaking off the memories, he stepped inside the room. 'What are you doing with Leonie?'

Bertrand looked up from his paperwork. 'Me?' His mouth twisted as if he was trying not to smile. 'What do you mean?'

Narrowing his eyes, Jacques stalked to a leather chair and sat down. 'You know exactly what I mean. I want you to stop.'

Bertrand tossed his pen onto the desk and leaned back. 'Why?'

'Why?' Jacques scowled. 'Francine wouldn't like it.'

'Francine can take care of herself. She doesn't need you to fight her battles for her.'

'So you admit that she has a battle to fight?'

'No.' Bertrand regarded him silently for a moment. 'But it really bothers you that I might be interested in Leonie, doesn't it? Yet you're not supposed to be serious.'

Jacques threw up his hands. 'All right, I admit that it bothers me.' He sent his brother a glare. 'But if that was what you wanted to know, you only had to ask me the question. You didn't have to…to…'

'Make you insanely jealous?'

'I'm not insanely jealous.'

Bertrand laughed. 'Oh, yes, you are. You should see your face when I go near her. Admit it, little brother, you're deeply in love.'

Clenching his jaw to prevent his response— any response—Jacques had no intention of sharing his feelings with his brother just so that he could mock him, because that was what this was all about.

Bertrand shook his head. 'I don't know why you are being so secretive. You need to stake your claim, let everyone know that she's yours.'

'Don't interfere, Bertrand.' He made an exasperated sound. 'I don't want Antoine to get the wrong idea. You know how quickly he will become attached to her if he thinks there's a chance of her becoming his stepmother, and I don't want him to be heartbroken when she leaves.'

Bertrand's face lost its teasing expression. 'You mean, *if* she leaves.'

'When, not if.' He clenched his jaw again.

'But what about you? Won't you be heartbroken if she leaves? Why don't you ask her to stay?'

Jacques slumped in the chair, rubbing his forehead. 'She can't.'

'You've asked her?'

'She has a family of her own. She belongs with them.'

Bertrand frowned. 'But does she know that you want her to stay?'

Jacques hesitated. He recalled the moment when he'd almost asked her to stay, in the cellar, before they were interrupted. He hadn't had the opportunity to put it into words.

But then he also remembered how it was when they made love, and he believed he'd made himself clear without words. How could she not know?

'She knows,' he said flatly.

Bertrand's face fell. 'I'm sorry. I thought…'

'Thought what?' Jacques asked when his brother's voice trailed off.

'That you'd found the right woman for you at last, but that you wouldn't admit it. That you were allowing your past relationships to stop you opening your heart to her. I thought all I had to do was knock some sense into you by making you see how you felt about her. By making you jealous. But it's not that simple, is it?'

Jacques got to his feet with a sigh. 'No, it's not that simple, but I have accepted things as they are. I have no choice. So please, leave well alone.'

Nodding, Bertrand stood too. Before Jacques had figured out what he meant to do, his brother had enveloped him in a hug. 'I'm sorry, little brother. Truly. I wish this had worked out for you.'

He returned the hug. He wanted to say it was okay, but it wasn't. Not really. And besides, speech was difficult with a throat that wouldn't work. He pulled away, and left his brother's office. He needed to be alone for a while to put aside the emotion that had risen to the surface, thanks to Bertrand.

He hadn't needed his brother to point out how he would feel when Leonie left. It was something he would have to deal with when the time came. It was more important in the meantime to protect Antoine from being hurt.

After he'd walked around the winery and back to the house, he changed his mind about being alone, and went inside. He would be alone soon enough, since there was only a short time to go until Leonie left. He intended to make the most of that time.

* * *

The next morning, Leonie accompanied Jacques when he took Antoine to school. She helped Jacques unload the wheelchair from the van, then Antoine smiled at her. 'Will you still be here when I get home from school?'

'I think so.' She looked at Jacques.

He nodded, and ruffled Antoine's hair. 'We'll come and pick you up again, okay?'

'Okay. That's good.'

She smiled. She genuinely liked the boy, and not just because he was Jacques' son. She enjoyed his unique combination of enthusiasm and sensitivity. She could see similarities to both Kyle and Sam in him, but he wasn't exactly like either of them.

Once Antoine was safely inside the school, Jacques told her they were going for a drive to see some more of his beloved 'pays'—his home country. She was happy to hear it, and they set off. They passed through several pretty villages, and in one they came across a game of boules, and stopped to watch.

It was played on a flat piece of ground beneath the spreading branches of a tree, and they joined the dozen or so men who were observing the players—also men—leisurely pitching metal spheres at a small wooden ball.

'The cochonnet,' Jacques said, pointing at what she would have called the jack.

The players then began to argue over whose *boule* was the closest to the *cochonnet*, yet to her it looked obvious. After a few minutes, they left them to it and continued their tour. Passionate discussion was a tradition in *boules*, Jacques explained, and traditions were important in Provence.

They drove along the red-rock Gorges de Daluis with green torrents hundreds of metres below, then through the ski towns of Valberg and Beuil, and back down the Gorges du Cians.

They ate lunch at an impressive restaurant in the surprising town of Touët-sur-Var. The medieval town was literally stuck to a vertical cliff. Its very tall houses were tightly packed together, and many had an attic open to the elements, which in former times had been used for drying figs.

It was all fascinating to her, and she was glad she'd had the opportunity to see where Jacques had grown up. It was one of the many parts that went together to make up the whole of this amazing man. Before they got back into the van, she kissed him on the cheek, wishing she could tell him how she felt about him, but she knew she couldn't. It would complicate things for both of them, and maybe embarrass him as well.

He turned his head to capture her lips, then hugged her to him, and they stood there for several long moments, clinging to each other. In her head, in her heart, she told him how much she loved him. But not in words. That was something she'd never be able to do.

Later, they collected Antoine from school and took him back to the house, and, between them, helped him with his homework. When Antoine asked if she would come to stay again, she was noncommittal, replying that she hoped to see him again.

On the way back to Nice the next day, she asked, 'So, is Antoine coming to stay with us next weekend?'

'Yes.' He turned to her with a smile. 'I didn't tell him, though. I'll surprise him.'

'Excellent.' She grinned. 'We'll have to plan some interesting things to do while he's with us. We don't want him to get bored.'

Jacques sent her an odd look.

She arched her eyebrows. 'What?'

'You sound as if you're really pleased.'

Puzzled, she said, 'I am. Why shouldn't I be?'

He shook his head as he looked straight ahead again. 'No reason. It's just that…I have never met anyone like you. I've never known anyone want to spend time with Antoine, except for his family.'

She saw him swallow, as if the words had been difficult for him to utter. She squeezed his arm.

'Maybe you've never given anyone the chance.' She hesitated, then went on. 'You know, getting to know more people could be good for him.'

Jacques shrugged. 'It depends on the people.'

Tilting her head, she said, 'Not really. I know you didn't like the idea of wheelchair sports, but imagine how good it would be for him. The camaraderie of being part of a team for one thing, the self-esteem and the sheer fun too. Yes, he might get hurt from time to time, but in my experience boys seem to enjoy their bumps and bruises. I don't see why being in a wheelchair should make Antoine any different.'

He looked at her with one eyebrow raised. 'You had no intention of leaving that subject alone, did you?'

'No. Sorry if it annoys you, but that's just the way I am.'

His mouth curved. 'Persistent.'

'Only if I think I have a good point, and I do. You should let Antoine discover his own limitations.'

He said nothing more, and she let it drop for the time being.

She was glad to have Antoine's upcoming visit to focus on for the rest of the week. It stopped her from dwelling on the truth that she only had a short time left with Jacques, then she'd have to go home.

Home.

She did want to go home, of course she did. Sam and Kyle were there, weren't they? She loved them, and they needed her. It would be good to be back in her own house, with all her familiar things around her. She'd soon get into a routine, soon forget all about her stay in France.

No, she wouldn't. That wasn't what she wanted. She didn't want to forget a single thing. That would mean it had all been insignificant. And nothing about Jacques was insignificant.

She did not want to let her language skills slide either. To avoid this, she'd find a French conversation group, and hopefully she'd retain the expertise she'd managed to develop. And she'd store the precious memory of Jacques in a special place in her mind, to be brought out often and marvelled at.

For now, she didn't want to think about leaving, and Antoine's visit was a good distraction. What had Sam and Kyle enjoyed doing at his age? She had to think back a whole decade, but she remembered a certain family holiday when they'd stayed in a cabin with no electricity. The weather had been bad, so they'd spent a week inside, playing board games.

That had been a great week for family bonding and, as neither she nor Shane had played board games with their own parents, it had been as much fun for them as it had for the kids.

So, she took herself off to a department store to buy several board games. She stuck to those that seemed familiar because she didn't relish wading through a French instruction book. She also picked up a chess set because she could imagine Jacques and Antoine playing chess on future visits, when she wasn't around. She had no idea whether Jacques played, but if not they could learn together.

She convinced Jacques to convert an unused formal dining room into a downstairs bedroom for Antoine, shaking her head when Jacques told her that on previous visits he'd used an upstairs bedroom.

She went shopping again, this time returning with colourful posters for the bedroom walls, since they didn't have time to decorate. Jacques came into the room just as she was on a stepladder, sticking the last poster to the wall.

He ran a hand up one leg and she giggled. 'Don't, you'll make me fall.'

'I'll catch you. Then I'll carry you upstairs to bed and have my way with you.'

'Carry me? At your age? And put your back out just when Antoine is about to visit? Not a good idea.'

He laughed, shaking his head. 'You won't let me forget how old I am, will you? Have you finished here?'

'Yes. What do you think?'

'I think they lack artistic merit, but I also think he'll like what you have done to the room.'

'Good. That's what matters.'

She climbed down carefully, and his arms were already around her as she touched the ground. Turning, she leaned against him, and before she could stop them tears leaked from her eyes.

'What is it? What's wrong?' His horrified tone made her smile as she wiped away the tears with the back of her hand.

'Ignore me. There's nothing wrong.'

'How can I ignore you? I could never do that.'

'I mean, ignore the fact that I'm being silly.' She reached up for a kiss but he leaned back, out of reach.

'Tell me. Why are you crying?'

She sighed. He wasn't going to drop it, she could tell, and he'd called her persistent. 'It's just that…I've really enjoyed our time together and it's a shame that it has to end.'

His jaw twitched. 'It's not over yet.'

'No. But it will be, and quite soon.' She swiped at another stray tear.

'Could you… Is there any possibility that you might be able to stay longer?'

She hesitated. She'd thought about it. She'd thought long and hard. 'I'm afraid not.'

'Ah.' His arms still held her, but she felt him stiffen.

'It's not that I haven't considered it, but…I promised Sam and Kyle that I'd be home by mid-November.' She glanced up at him, then away. 'It's the anniversary of Shane's death then, you see. We always spend the day together. It's important to us…to the kids.'

She regretted putting such a deep frown on his face. 'Anyway, don't worry, I'm perfectly all right about it. About leaving, I mean.'

'Are you?'

'Of course.' She couldn't bear him to think she was going to make a scene, when she'd known all along that their relationship was just temporary. Clearing her throat, she said, 'I'm dying to see Sam and Kyle again.'

'I'm sure you are.' He nodded, but he was still frowning, so she pasted on her brightest smile.

'We should make the most of the time we have left. You know, make some special memories.' She wriggled in his arms in an attempt to lighten the mood. 'We could go upstairs and start now.'

His breath hissed out as his eyes closed, and his hold on her tightened. 'I will never forget you.'

'I know.' For a moment, she fought to keep the tears back, then she took a deep breath. 'It's going to be hard to say goodbye, but it's not as if we have a choice, is it? And it's what we always planned.'

Jacques nodded. He did not mean to make a fool of himself by blurting out that he wanted her to stay. Nor did he want to make leaving harder on her than it had to be, so, although he desperately wanted to tell Leonie how he felt about her, he wouldn't.

He would put his own feelings aside and do what she needed him to do, which was to make their parting as easy as possible, and to go along with what she was saying now.

'You're right. It will be fine. We always knew we would have to say goodbye.'

He stroked her cheek, smoothed back her hair while looking into her beautiful blue eyes, then, with one arm behind her back, he bent to reach behind her knees, and swung her into his arms. 'I am *not* too old to carry you upstairs.'

She squealed, but let her head drop back, laughing. It was good to see her laughter after the tears of a few moments before, and he backed towards the door.

Later, when Leonie was sleeping, her head resting on his chest, he imagined his life once she'd gone.

It would go on. He knew that much. He'd even date again. Perhaps. One day.

But even as he imagined bringing some other woman to the villa, he felt a curdling sensation in his stomach, like sour milk.

He shut down the image abruptly. In its place, he breathed in the clean, sweet scent of her skin and let it fill his senses.

When they'd started this relationship, his goal had been to make her happy in the short term—himself too, of course—but he hadn't wanted anything beyond that. Now, though…now he did want more, and he knew he could never have it. This was the reason for the raw ache at the back of his throat.

If he said anything, if he gave her any indication that he wanted her to stay, he would make things more difficult than they needed to be. And she didn't deserve that. She deserved their split to be easy, as comfortable as he could possibly make it.

So, this was his new goal. To get through her departure without weakening, to make it possible for her to leave with a smile on her face.

Antoine loved the board games. Leonie grinned at the success of her plan, even as she pretended to cry over the loss of her property empire. They played for hours, the three of them, late into the night. And the next day, after a slow start, Leonie asked him what he'd most like to do. He told her that he wanted to go into the ocean.

She relayed the information to Jacques, who'd just joined them. 'So, you have to take him into the water,' she said. She had no intention of wearing a swimsuit.

Jacques winked at Antoine. 'Only if you'll come in with us,' he said, a hint of challenge in his eyes.

'Me?' She grimaced, but when she tried to use the fact that she didn't own a suit as an excuse, Jacques and Antoine ganged up on her.

'Okay, okay, I'll go and buy one,' she grumbled.

She was still reluctant when the time came to strip off and let everyone see her body. It was one thing to feel gorgeous when alone in bed with Jacques, it was quite another to flaunt her wobbly bits on a popular beach.

It was a logistical exercise to get Antoine into the water, but they managed it between them, as she'd known they would. And his delighted face made the effort and embarrassment worthwhile.

Leonie cooked dinner that night, finding her way around Jacques' kitchen without difficulty, and she was thrilled when both Jacques and Antoine praised her simple stir-fry.

Antoine was ready for bed not long after they'd

finished eating. Swimming had tired him out, but he refused to give in. Yawning, he sat on the terrace with them while they finished a bottle of wine. He'd brought up the topic of wheelchair sport earlier in the day, and now he mentioned it again.

Leonie smiled. 'I think it's great that you want to have a go,' she said, hoping Jacques would come round to the idea.

'I have been looking into clubs and facilities,' Jacques said. 'I will get some more information this week, I promise. Whatever you want to do, I will see if it can be arranged.'

'That's fantastic.' She gave him her warmest smile, thrilled that he'd changed his attitude. 'And, you know, if it turns out that you don't like it, you don't have to keep on with it,' she said to Antoine.

Antoine grinned. 'Do you think I could be in the paralympics one day?'

'You can do anything you want to do,' Leonie said firmly. 'You just have to have a dream, and then go for it. You'll have your setbacks just like everybody does, but if you want something badly enough, you keep trying. You dream, you work, you struggle, you fail, and you try again, until you succeed.'

He yawned again. 'Okay.'

'Come on, it's time for bed,' Jacques said, getting to his feet. 'You've had an exhausting day.'

'But it's been great.'

When Jacques put his hand tenderly on his son's shoulder, she looked at his face and saw the raw emotion there. A muscle twitched in his cheek, and she saw him swallow. 'Yes, it has, hasn't it? We have to thank Leonie for that.'

Leonie looked from father to son and back again, her heart battering her rib cage. She had to bite her lip to keep from shouting out that she loved both of them.

'Can we do this again?' Antoine asked.

Leonie glanced at Jacques. 'Next weekend is my last. I'll be going home on Monday,' she explained to Antoine.

His face fell.

'Don't worry, I'm sure your dad will arrange for you to come here more often in future.'

'But it won't be the same without you.'

Jacques turned away.

She patted Antoine's hand. 'Your dad will be here. That's the main thing.'

When Antoine was settled in bed, they returned to the terrace. As she went to sit in her usual chair Jacques caught her wrist and pulled her onto his lap. Rather than worry about his legs going numb, she curled into his chest, the cool cotton fabric of his shirt smooth against her cheek.

His chin rested lightly on the top of her head. 'Thank you,' he whispered.

He said no more, but she didn't need to ask him what he was referring to. She hadn't done anything special, nothing that he couldn't have done without her, but she'd been the agitator who stirred up the status quo and made him see possibilities.

She smiled into his chest. He was very welcome.

CHAPTER ELEVEN

LEONIE had arranged to meet Jacques at Jean-Claude's café that afternoon, but first she wanted to pop across the street to see Chantal. She'd spent very little time in her apartment over the last couple of weeks and this morning, when she'd opened the doors to her balcony after returning from school—another place she hadn't spent much time recently—she'd been surprised to see Chantal's shutters closed and no sign of her friend.

She hurried through the few chores she'd been meaning to do, then got ready to go out. She took another look across the street before closing the doors again. Why would Chantal not be sitting at her window? She didn't go out in the afternoon; once she'd done her morning shopping, that was it for the day.

Glancing around her apartment as she slipped on her shoes, she wondered how she could ever have thought it was anything but lovely. Small, true, but big enough for her. It had been absolutely perfect as a base, and she would be sad to hand back the keys.

Across the street, when she couldn't raise Chantal she told herself not to worry, that she was just out shopping. But relief rolled over her when she pushed open the café door and the first person she saw was Chantal. Sitting on a bar stool, legs swinging, she looked ten—no, twenty—years younger, at least.

Leonie dashed over and gave her a hug. 'I'm so glad you're all right.'

Chantal's eyebrows rose. 'Why? What did you think had happened to me?'

'I was trying not to think about the possibilities. I'm used to seeing you at the window. When you weren't there…' She settled on a stool alongside her.

'Ah, well, you've been away so much recently, I haven't had a chance to tell you.'

'Tell me what?' Her eyes went to the café door as it opened, searching for Jacques, but it wasn't him. She brought her attention back to her friend.

'Jean-Claude and I are getting married.'

She gaped. 'Oh, my. This is sudden.'

Chantal laughed. 'We don't have a lot of time to waste. We're not getting any younger. When you know something is right, you have to grab it with both hands and make the most of it.'

'And you…you know this is right?'

'Yes.'

Leonie saw the certainty in her eyes. 'Then I'm very happy for you.' She slipped off the stool and gave her another hug.

By the time she let go, Jacques had arrived and he was stunned at the news, but pleased for his old friend. He slapped Jean-Claude on the back and wished him happiness, although from the size of the smile on his face Leonie didn't think he was in need of any extra.

A wave of envy flowed right through her. Life wasn't fair. She didn't begrudge these two people one smidgen of their new-found love and happiness, but she'd also found love, and she didn't get to enjoy a happy ending.

She made an effort to shake off this resentment because it was completely unjustified and spoiling her enjoyment of what should be a happy moment.

Once the congratulations and questions and exclamations had died down, Leonie and Jacques moved off to a table at the other side of the café.

'It's been a while since we've been here,' she said, settling in her chair.

'Yes. And this is where it all started.'

She looked up at his tone. It was wistful, and almost sad. 'You don't regret meeting me, do you?'

He shook his head. 'You know I don't. But I do regret…'

'What?' She held her breath.

He seemed to be considering and discarding his words. Eventually, he shrugged. 'That your stay is almost over.'

'Yes.' She stared into the dark depths of her coffee. 'I do too.'

'But we still have this weekend, and I think we should make it a good one.'

'Oh, yes, I agree.' She smiled, already imagining the bone-melting satisfaction she'd feel at his hands at night. 'What do you suggest?'

'Well, this for Sunday.' He took some tickets from his jacket pocket and held them out for her to see.

'A ballet?' she said, surprised.

He nodded. 'I thought you would like to see a ballet. You mentioned once that you'd never done so. But if you don't want to go, it's not a problem.' He returned the tickets to his pocket.

'I think it's a lovely idea, it's just not what I expected.'

He looked at her for a long moment. 'Leonie… I…'

She loved that after all this time, he still said her

name differently from anyone else. She would soon have to get used to not hearing it. She had to push away that thought before it made her teary and emotional. She'd be fighting a constant battle against tears for the next week.

Just as Jacques opened his mouth to continue her phone rang. She jerked upright. It had to be Sam. She held up her hand. 'Hold that thought, okay?'

After retrieving the phone from her bag, she checked the display and quickly pushed the button.

'Sammi!' She grinned at Jacques and he smiled too. Leaning back in his chair, he picked up his cup, signalling that she should go ahead and chat. She put a hand over her free ear to hear what Sam was saying. 'What? Oh, the noise? I'm in a café.'

'Who are you with?' Sam asked.

Leonie glanced at Jacques. 'I'm with a friend.'

'So you did manage to make a friend, then?'

'Yes, I did. A good friend.' She swallowed. Oh, goodness, if Sam knew what she'd been getting up to, she'd be horrified. She would never in a million years expect her mother to sleep with a stranger, someone who wasn't her father.

But she wouldn't find out. Leonie screwed up her eyes. *She* would never tell her, that was for sure, and there was no chance she would hear it from anyone else.

'That's super, Mum. Will you keep in touch, do you think? Maybe she'll be able to come over here for a holiday later.'

'Um…maybe.' She knew her cheeks had turned red, even though Sam couldn't see her. 'But I doubt it.'

'Oh…well, never mind. At least you've had a good time. You *have* had a good time, haven't you, Mum?'

'Yes. Oh, yes, I have.'

'That's great because I can't wait for you to come home.'

'I'm looking forward to coming home too.' She bit the inside of her cheek as she finished speaking. It was true, on one level. On another, she was utterly dreading it, but Sam didn't need to know that and she never would.

Out of the corner of her eye she saw Jacques' head lift at her words, but his expression didn't change.

'How's Kyle?'

'He's…he's fine. Same as always.'

Leonie frowned at the phone. Was it her imagination, or had Sam hesitated? 'Are you sure?'

'You know Kyle,' Sam went on. 'He's a pain in the proverbial.'

Leonie laughed, then cleared her throat so that she could speak past a lump of emotion. 'It seems ages since I saw you both.'

'I know. Not long now, though. Have you arranged your return flight?'

'Yes, it's been arranged for a while.' Actually, she'd made the return booking when she'd organised the flight over. It had seemed important then to make sure that nothing would prevent her returning on time. Now, she almost wished the flight would be cancelled.

No, that wasn't true.

Yes, it was.

Oh, her heart hurt from flip-flopping between the two choices. Not that there was a choice, really. She was going home and that was that.

'Well, I'd better get off the phone,' Sam said. 'These bills are killing me.'

'Oh, Sam, don't be silly. You know I'll help you out with the phone bill. It's for my sake that you're calling after all.'

'Mine too. I've missed you, Mum.'

'Oh.' Tears immediately filled her eyes. Such sweet words from her sweet girl. 'I've missed you too, honey.' She sniffed. 'I can't wait to see you.'

After they'd said their goodbyes, she returned the phone to her bag and pulled out a tissue to wipe her eyes.

Jacques gave her a look of concern.

'Don't worry,' she said. 'I'm just being a mum. This is what we do.'

'It wasn't bad news?'

'No, no. Quite the opposite. Sam just told me she can't wait for me to get home.' She gave him a shaky smile. 'Of course, that probably means she's sick of doing the laundry and the cooking and that Kyle's made a mess of the house. But that's okay, it's nice to know that I'm needed.'

Jacques was silent, staring at her tearful face.

'So, what were you going to say before the phone rang?'

'Hmm?' He shook his head. 'No, it was nothing.'

His heart was pounding against his ribs. He'd been so close to telling her how he felt. Again! He could hardly believe he'd again been on the point of saying it when her phone had rung. Hadn't he vowed to make her leaving as easy on her as he could? He had to remember that.

The call had been a well-timed reminder that she wouldn't…couldn't stay. He would have to say goodbye and wish her well for the future without ever letting her know how much it hurt him to do so.

If she knew, she would be anxious on his behalf. That was the type of person she was. If she had any idea how much she meant to him, she wouldn't be able to walk away and get on with her life without worrying about him. And he didn't want that for her. He wanted her to go on to find happiness, even if that meant finding someone else to share her life.

Pain pierced his chest and buried itself in his stomach.

She might find someone else.

He knew she'd loved her husband, but he could handle that. It was different. He was her past and, as she'd said, her life with him was part of her. But the thought of another man being her future…he didn't know whether he could handle that thought. It was better not to think about it at all. To just say goodbye. To choose emotional numbness over feeling too much.

Over the next few days, Leonie seemed to be continually saying goodbye. First came the end of the course and weepy farewells all round. They all swapped e-mail addresses and promised to keep in touch, but Leonie knew they wouldn't. Perhaps one or two of the younger ones would correspond for a while, but the most she expected to do was send a group greeting at Christmas, which wasn't that far away, come to think of it.

Then there was Chantal. She managed to catch her on one of the rare occasions she was home to hand over a gift. Intended to be a combined parting and wedding present, it was a beautiful silk robe based on a vintage design, demure and feminine. Chantal loved it, and Leonie congratulated herself on finding something that didn't offend the style sense of this elegant lady. They hugged as they wished each other a wonderful life.

Next she dropped into the café to say goodbye to Jean-Claude, and to some of his regular customers who'd become almost-friends during the time she'd been there.

And then it was time to think about Jacques, and what would be their last outing together.

The ballet was everything Leonie had imagined it would be. It was held at the nineteenth-century opera house on the edge of the old town. Decked out in sumptuous red velvet, crystal chandeliers and lots of gold, it was the perfect venue, Leonie decided, for such a momentous occasion.

Not that anyone would recognise it as such, except the two of them.

She was wearing her beautiful blue dress for the last time. Once home, she would pack it away, never to be worn again. It would not feel right to wear it for any other occasion, with any other person.

She'd put up her hair again, attempting the

same style as the hairdresser, but this time it looked less precarious whereas, in truth, it was far more so. Still, Jacques had complimented her on it, and as soon as they reached his villa it would be coming down anyway.

A glance around the theatre had told her that it wasn't the sort of place where she could cuddle up to Jacques while they watched the stage performance, so she sat perfectly still as she slid a sideways look at him. He half turned his head and gave her a quick smile.

He was looking particularly gorgeous tonight in a tuxedo, and awe filled her at just how lucky she had been to meet him, this man she couldn't resist, and whose bed she couldn't wait to share. A shiver trickled down her spine as she turned back to face the stage. Waiting would only make it all the better when the time came.

Later, Jacques brought her a glass of wine, and she sipped it where she stood at the edge of his balcony, wondering whether she'd be able to buy Domaine Broussard wine in Australia. If not, it would be one of many, many things she would miss.

She'd miss this villa with its sparkling night-time views of the city. She'd miss the strength of his arms as they encircled her. And she'd miss being a person in her own right, because that was what she'd been here. Not someone's mum, but a sexy, desirable woman.

Her lips curved, not quite achieving a smile—she was too sad for that. She hoped she didn't look as sad as she felt.

Jacques looked bleak.

And her imminent departure loomed between them like an uninvited third person.

'The ballet was lovely,' she said in an effort to start a conversation.

'Yes.'

They lapsed into silence again.

'We always knew this time would come,' she said after several moments.

'Yes.' Jacques placed his glass on the broad balustrade. 'But we don't have to like it.'

'No.'

He reached into his suit jacket and pulled out an envelope. 'While I think of it. Put this in your handbag.'

After waiting for her to put her glass down next to his, he handed it over. 'No, don't open it now,' he said when she went to slide a finger under the flap.

'What is it?'

'Just some French language practice I've written out for you.'

She was surprised, but nodded. 'I was thinking

that I might join a French conversation group. I'm sure I'll be able to find one locally.'

'That's a good idea.' He watched her push the envelope deep into her handbag. 'When you join the group, this would be a good time to read it.'

'Okay. Thank you.'

He took her in his arms. 'I'm going to miss you. I know I've already said it, but I don't know what else to say.'

'I know.' She sniffed. 'I'll miss you too. And I promised myself I wouldn't cry, so no more talk of missing each other, okay? Let's be positive.'

'Okay.' He took just one of the pins from her hair and, as if it had been waiting for his permission, it tumbled down. 'Meeting you is the best thing that's ever happened to me. I am positive of that.'

She swallowed. 'We still have tonight, Jacques. We should make the most of it, don't you think?'

He touched his lips to hers. 'I am positive that we will.'

It was late when she woke the next day, and Leonie was sure her veins were filled with champagne. Certainly nothing as substantial as blood. And her muscles were so relaxed it was a wonder she could stand.

But stand she did, because she had to shower and dress and return to her apartment to collect her baggage, then leave for the airport. There was no time for anything else, however tempting it might be to curl against Jacques' back and nibble his neck, to slide her hands over his skin and wake him with a whispered suggestion in his ear.

He woke just as she finished getting dressed. He looked at the clock, then sat up and went to get out of bed.

'No.' Leonie held out a hand. 'Stay there. This is how I want to leave.'

'What? But…the airport. I will drive you there.'

'No. Please. I've been thinking and I can't stand the idea of saying goodbye to you in an airport, surrounded by other people. I don't want that.'

She smiled sadly, and moved to the side of the bed. 'I don't want to say goodbye at all. I want to kiss you, and leave you in bed, as if I'm only going shopping, or something. Please. Humour me. It will be easier for me this way.'

She bent over him as she spoke, then kissed him on the lips. 'I'm off. Have a good day.'

Jacques took hold of her head with gentle hands and gave her a kiss that was so full of tenderness, she felt tears spring to her eyes despite her determination not to cry.

'Have a wonderful…day.' He dropped a final kiss on the top of her head, then let her go.

She straightened, exhaled and pulled back her

shoulders. With no more words, and no further glances in his direction as much as she wanted to steal one last look, she left the villa.

Jacques winced at the sound of the door closing, signalling that she'd gone. He'd restrained himself from running after her, from shouting, *Don't go!*

He had to let her go without a fuss. It was the right thing to do. It was what he had promised himself he would do. But it didn't feel right. It felt like the worst moment of his life. And there was nothing he could do about it. He just had to accept it, and hope that one day the memory of their time together would become hazy, like a faded photograph.

Thinking about the letter he'd written, he sighed. It had to be enough. When she read it, she would know how much she had meant to him.

Back at her apartment, and glad that she'd done almost all of her packing the day before, Leonie tucked her blue dress and evening accessories into her suitcase, then dressed in the comfortable travelling clothes she'd left out.

While she went through the motions of transporting herself and her baggage to the airport, checking in and buying a coffee, she was fine. It was when she stopped, when she had nothing to do but remember where she was, and who she was leaving behind, that her composure cracked.

She'd had to make several trips to the ladies' room to wash her face by the time her flight was announced, but still, she felt she'd made the right decision in electing not to say goodbye to Jacques at the airport.

She would have been in no fit state to board if she'd had to go through such a heart-wrenching scene. And what kind of image of her would it have left him with? No, she preferred the way they'd done it, parting on a high note, with the memory of their mind-blowing final night uppermost in his mind.

CHAPTER TWELVE

'MUM!'

Leonie looked up as she stepped from the taxi. 'Sammi!'

The driver had unloaded her bags and driven off by the time she pulled back from hugging her daughter. 'Oh, sweetie, it's so good to see you.'

'Good to be home?'

She swallowed the lump that threatened to make a liar of her. 'Yes, absolutely.'

'Well, let's get all this stuff inside.' Sam grabbed a trolley case and a small bag, and headed for the house.

Leonie managed to gather everything else and followed her. 'Where's Kyle? He could have helped.'

'He's…well, he's not here.'

'Charming. You'd think he could have made the effort to be here to welcome his mum home. Then again, if it means he's taking his studies seriously, I suppose I'm pleased, really. I'll see him tonight.'

Sam made a low humming noise and dragged the suitcase into her mother's bedroom.

Leonie looked from side to side as she went. 'Goodness, I didn't expect this.'

'Expect what?' Sam asked from inside the room.

'That the house would be so clean and tidy. What did you do—employ a firm of cleaners to come in and sort it out before I got home?'

Sam looked a little offended. 'I'm not totally useless, Mum. I do know how to do housework.'

Leonie dropped an armful of bags on the bed. 'I know, sweetheart. But you have a busy life, studying as well as volunteering. I didn't expect you to spend all your free time working on the house.' She unzipped a bag and right at the top were the lavender toiletries she'd bought at the *vendange* festival. She grabbed them and headed for the ensuite bathroom, trying to ignore the strong scent. 'And, besides, I know Kyle, and I know what a mess he leaves wherever he goes,' she said on her way back to the bed. 'I don't suppose he helped, did he?'

'Well…not really.' Sam looked away. 'I'd better put the kettle on. I bet you're dying for a cup of coffee. I'll have one ready for when you've freshened up. That's if you can still stomach instant coffee now that you've been living amongst the glitterati?' She looked over her shoulder, grinning, as she moved towards the door.

'Actually, I'll have tea, please.' Although Sam had been joking, Leonie wasn't sure that she could stomach instant coffee after the heavenly, aromatic coffee she was used to at Jean-Claude's café.

'Sure.' Sam disappeared.

She'd have to invest in one of those espresso machines that were all the rage and which she'd never seen the point of, till now. Leonie found her cosmetic bag and returned to the ensuite where she stared at herself in the mirror.

Now that she was alone, she could take the time to inspect the damage from the long, long flight. It had had the effect of making her look older. At least, she hoped it was just the flight and therefore temporary. She hoped it wasn't the result of the emptiness she felt at knowing she'd never see Jacques again.

'Kettle's boiled,' Sam called, and Leonie jerked herself out of the semi-trance she'd fallen into. She would look and feel better by the next day, she was sure of it.

'So, tell me all about it,' Sam said, once they were settled on either side of the kitchen table. 'And do you speak French like a native now?'

'Not like a native, no,' she said with a laugh, 'but I can get by.'

'Was it everything you thought it would be?'

'Oh, more so. It was much more than I could have imagined.'

'You sound quite dreamy, Mum. If I didn't know you well, I could think you'd fallen in love with the place, or something.'

Shocked, Leonie pulled herself up. 'If I sound dreamy, it's because I'm tired,' she said briskly.

'Relax, Mum.' Sam laughed. 'I *do* know you well, remember?'

'Right.' Leonie took a drink of tea, hiding behind the mug for a moment while she gathered her thoughts. 'Well, actually, I did fall in love with Nice, or, rather, with France, and the French.'

'So, come on, Mum, tell me all about it.'

'What shall I tell you about?' She took another sip of tea. 'Oh, I saw Monte Carlo, and St Tropez, and Cannes. I have photos on my phone to show you all of those places. And I…um…went to a winery.'

'Wow. And you did all this on your own? Or did you go sightseeing with your friend, the one you told me about?'

'With my friend.' She rubbed her forehead. 'I'll tell you more when I'm not feeling so jet-lagged. My mind feels like it's full of cotton wool.'

'Sure.' Sam hesitated, then took a deep breath.

'Mum, I was going to wait till you'd been back a bit longer, but I guess I have to do this now. It's not going to get any easier if I wait.'

'Do what?' Leonie's stomach clenched with apprehension. The look on Sam's face told her to expect something serious.

'Kyle…isn't at university.'

Leonie put down her mug and pressed her hands flat on the table. 'Where is he? Is he in trouble? Is he hurt?'

'No, no, nothing like that. He's finished with uni. He's dropped out, because he's decided what he wants to do with his life.'

Leonie stared. 'What do you mean?'

'He's joined the army.'

'He's what?' She frowned. 'Doesn't he need my permission to do something like that?'

'No, Mum. Believe it or not, he's an adult. He doesn't need anybody's permission. He passed the interview and the medical, and the physical test and everything, and they signed him up.'

It took a moment for Sam's words to sink in and by then Leonie's stomach was rolling. 'He's already joined up? I don't get to talk to him about it first?'

Sam shook her head. 'He's already doing his training at a camp in Wagga Wagga.'

'Wagga Wagga? But that's hours away. When will I see him again?'

'When he has leave, I guess, but that could be some time yet.'

Leonie sank against the back of the chair. 'I can't believe you didn't tell me before now. I wish I'd had the chance to talk to him.'

'He didn't want me to tell you, Mum. He didn't want you to try to talk him out of it.'

'But…if it's truly what he wants…I wouldn't try to talk him out of it. I only want to be sure he knows what he's doing.'

Sam nodded. 'You have to trust him, Mum. I talked to him, and it sounded to me like he was fully committed. He didn't have any doubts. And you have to admit, it's a good fit really. Just the right job for him.'

'Oh.' She took a couple of deep breaths. 'I suppose so.' Memories of her little boy, the image of his father, crowded into her mind. He'd always been adventurous, a daredevil, but with a strong sense of right and wrong, and an urge to protect anyone weaker than himself. 'All right, I admit it. But will I at least be able to talk to him by phone?'

Sam nodded again. 'He's going to call you. He plans to let you get used to the idea first, then he'll ring.'

Leonie gave a rueful smile. 'I'd better get used to the idea pretty quickly, then, hadn't I?' She finished her tea, then sighed. 'So, honey, it's just you and me here from now on. I'll be able to cook what Kyle calls "girlie food". No more complaints about salad, eh?'

Sam pulled her bottom lip between her teeth, then said, 'About that…'

'What? About what? Salad?'

'About it being just the two of us…'

Leonie's eyes widened. 'You don't have plans to move someone into Kyle's room, do you? I mean, it might be okay, but—'

'No, no, not that. It's about me…and university.'

'Don't tell me you're dropping out too. Oh, Sam, no.'

'Not dropping out, no. I'm deferring.'

'Deferring?'

'Taking a year off.'

'I know what it means. Oh, well, Sammi, you've always been such a hard worker, maybe it will do you good to have a bit of a holiday. We could do some things together, mother and daughter stuff. It will be nice.' She smiled. 'That wasn't such bad news after all.'

'Mum, the thing is…I'm taking a year off to go overseas. I've already found a job as an aid worker.'

Leonie covered her mouth with her hand. 'No,' she murmured into her palm.

'Yes. It was easier for me to find a place because of the volunteer work I've done.'

She saw the light in her daughter's eyes, and drew in a deep breath. 'Where are you going?'

'Africa. A place called Chad.'

'But that's dangerous.'

'I'll be careful. Look, I know it's a bit of a shock, especially with both of us moving out at the same time like this, but it wasn't intentional, it just worked out that way, and it did have to happen sometime.'

Sam chewed her lip again. 'I really want to do this, Mum. Please be happy for me. It's only a year, then I'll be back and wanting your help again.'

'No, you won't. After a year as an aid worker, you'll be completely independent. You won't want to live with your old mum again.'

Sam made an ambiguous sound in her throat and Leonie knew she was right. In one blow, she'd lost both of her babies, and she wasn't ready for it.

Her nest was empty.

'Why did you say you wanted me to come home?'

Her eyes wide, Sam said, 'Because I did, of course. I missed you, and I didn't want you to think we didn't need you.'

'But you don't need me.' She said it without any accusation in her tone, just stating a fact. 'You managed perfectly well without me, and you will continue to manage perfectly well without me.'

Sam fidgeted with her mug.

'When do you leave?' Leonie asked after several seconds of silence.

'End of this week.'

So soon. She nodded. 'I'm proud of you. I don't want you to go and I'm going to miss you like crazy, but I am proud of you. I love you.'

'Thanks, Mum.' Sam came around the table and hugged her from behind. 'You're terrific. I love you too.' As she straightened, she said, 'I hate leaving you alone, but I hope you'll get out and meet people. Join some clubs or something, okay?'

Oh, yes, those clubs. What should she do? Gardening? Pottery? T'ai chi?

After checking that Sam had left the kitchen, she let out a mighty sigh. Talk about conflicting emotions. She had so much going on inside it was a wonder she had any energy left to breathe.

Apart from the obvious worries about both her son's and daughter's choice of occupation, and the fact that she wouldn't see either of them for ages, there was the knowledge that she'd left Jacques because she was needed at home, and now it turned out that she wasn't needed here after all.

On the one hand, she was glad she hadn't known about both Kyle's and Sam's plans earlier or she would have cut short her stay in France to rush home and talk to them about their choices. On the other, if she'd known that her role was going to become redundant as soon as she returned…would she have wanted to come home at all?

Her mind was still in turmoil when she saw Sam off on her big adventure. In a way, she envied her daughter. If she hadn't married Shane and settled straight into the role of wife and mother, she might have done something similar herself. But her life had gone in a different direction, and she didn't regret a moment of it.

She drove home from the airport, a short journey, and parked her car in the driveway. She sat there for a long time, looking at her spacious suburban house. This was a home for a family, with children who would use the play equipment that Shane had erected in the backyard, dig in the sandpit and splash in the pool in summer.

The house was far too big for her, but when she'd mentioned that she might sell it Sam had been shocked and totally against the idea.

What was she going to do with herself here all alone?

Maybe she should take a leaf out of Sam's

book and do some volunteering. It might help her to feel needed.

She'd read an article about volunteering some time ago. The journalist had contended that people could find their soul mates amongst their fellow volunteers, since they were like-minded people with similar values.

It was a good theory, and she was sure it worked for some, but she wasn't interested in meeting someone like her. She'd fallen in love with Jacques because he was *different*.

The admission caused a jolt to her heart, but it was the truth. In this case, different was good. So very, very good.

She'd been rattling around in the big, empty house for several days before Kyle finally called. It was great to talk to him, and he was so enthusiastic about his new life that she knew she wouldn't have a hope of talking him out of it. Not that she wanted to. She'd come to terms with the knowledge that her children were no longer children and she had to let them go off on their own paths.

She told him she was proud of him and that his father would have been proud too, then she hung up.

Neither Kyle nor Sam, who'd phoned that morning to say she'd arrived in Chad and was fine, had mentioned the significance of the date.

She knew that neither of them had forgotten their father, but they had both moved on. They no longer felt the need to commemorate that sad day.

She looked around her home. It didn't feel like her home any longer. She felt like an interloper, someone pretending to be a suburban housewife. Perhaps it was time to have a big clean-up, to clear out much of the clutter. The last time she'd tried to de-clutter, she'd found herself wanting to keep every item because of the memories they held. She didn't expect that to be a problem this time.

But before she did that she'd go to the library and research the possibility of joining a French language group. If she couldn't find one, maybe she could even start one herself.

The thought reminded her of the envelope that Jacques had given her before she'd left Nice. With all that had been happening since her return, she'd forgotten about it.

In the bedroom, she pulled out the bag, found the envelope and slit it open with her nail. But as soon as she opened the single sheet of paper, she realised that it wasn't quite what Jacques had led her to believe.

It was a letter.

She flopped back against the pillows, her heart in her throat as she began to read.

* * *

When she'd finished reading, her pillow was drenched. All the tears she'd stoically stored up since the day she'd walked away from Jacques had now been released.

He loved her.

She closed her eyes, remembering every detail of his face as it had been on that last day, his voice, the trembling of his hands as he held her head, his kiss.

Of course he loved her. She should have known. Instead, she'd walked away, leaving behind her destiny.

It was a long time before she could bring herself to sit up. When she did, it was to acknowledge that this bedroom represented her past, and it was time to make a decision about her future.

She remembered Chantal telling her that when something seemed right, you had to grab it and not waste time. Being with Jacques had felt right. Even with distance between them, she could only think of being with him as thoroughly right.

Why hadn't she seized the opportunity to stay with him?

Because he hadn't asked her.

But he hadn't asked her because he'd known she couldn't stay. The truth was that now there was nothing stopping her from going back.

Her breath left her lungs at the thought of it,

and she clung to the edge of the bed as if she might fall.

They hadn't even exchanged phone numbers at the end. Nor e-mail addresses. That was how certain they'd been that her departure meant the end of their relationship. But she knew how to find him.

Jacques had been so definite about never marrying again. But that was because he couldn't trust women after what had happened in his past. She understood. He said he loved her, but if she gave up everything to move there on a permanent basis, she would want a commitment from him. That was only fair, wasn't it?

But then, what did she really have to give up?

It wasn't as if either of her kids would need a home with her in the near future. She could even move to France and not tell them; they'd never know the difference as long as she kept her mobile phone number.

She let out a short laugh. Not that she would do something so crazy. Of course she'd tell them, but she didn't have to sell the house, not immediately. She could rent it out to a young family who would once again fill it with the sounds of childish laughter.

And renting out the house would help to offset the extra expense of a small apartment in Nice, which meant that she could move there as an independent woman. Then, if Jacques wasn't ready to make a commitment, she could wait. If he didn't already know he could trust her, he would learn in time that he could.

She stood, excitement starting to bubble in her veins. She could do this, and when Sam returned from overseas the house would be available for her if she wanted it.

The more she thought about it, the more she knew that she'd finished with her life here. She'd been reborn in France; well, reinvented anyway. She was a different person now. The last thing she could see herself doing was joining one of those clubs and becoming old before her time.

But she *could* see herself strolling beside the Mediterranean on the Promenade des Anglais, maybe getting up early to visit the flower market, or dropping into Jean-Claude's café for a cup of the best coffee she'd ever tasted.

And could she see herself with Jacques for ever?

Oh, yes. Without a single doubt. She was ready to commit to him. And to Antoine too, because they came as a package. She was well aware that she'd be taking on the full-time care of his son, and she was more than ready. It would feel good to be needed again.

She knew there would be more to the move than simply a change of location. She'd have to grow accustomed to the cultural differences that would affect the smallest aspects of her life. She knew, for instance, that it was considered impolite to bite into a slice of bread in a restaurant, that she would be expected to break it into small pieces before eating it. Jacques had taught her that, and she'd laughed, unable to see what was so wrong with her way. But she accepted that this was only one example of the multitude of minor adjustments she'd have to make. She would always be an outsider, not quite at home. But then, she wasn't at home in Australia now either. Not without Jacques.

She'd made the decision that she was going to spend her future in Nice, and that was what she would do whether things worked out with Jacques or not. She hoped they would, of course, but she was prepared to make the move regardless. She loved Jacques, but if he decided that he couldn't take the risk of marrying her, she would live alone in a little apartment in Nice.

She had friends there. Chantal and Jean-Claude. Okay, two wasn't a huge number, but it compared favourably with zero, which was how many friends she had here. She and Shane had been a couple for so long that any friends they'd made were *their* friends, and, logically, most of them were couples too. Since Shane had died, she'd lost contact with all of them.

She was sure it was unintentional on their part, it was just a fact that a single, widowed woman didn't fit into their social circle. It was natural for them to stop including her in their activities.

But Chantal and Jean-Claude were *her* friends. She'd made them all on her own, and she would make more. She would create a life for herself. She would create a future.

It took a few weeks to organise everything to her satisfaction, to find suitable tenants, a trustworthy property manager, and to deal with the changeover of billing for utilities and so on. Mundane and frustrating activities when all she wanted to do was jump on a plane and see Jacques again, but she had to do this right if she was going to do it at all.

The wait was made all the more frustrating by the dreams she'd started having again. Just like those she'd had before she'd slept with Jacques for the first time.

It was as if her body missed him and was trying to fill his absence with the fantasy of him. Each morning when she woke, she could almost feel his body curled protectively around hers, his skin against her skin, his breath on her neck.

When she started to pack up the house, she knew the move was finally happening, and this was when it really hit her that she was moving on in every way possible. All the memories her family had created together in this home were being packed into boxes and sent into storage.

One day, maybe, Sam or Kyle would unpack those boxes and be reminded of their happy childhood—because it had been a happy childhood, she had no doubt of it. She and Shane had been good parents and a close-knit team. She need have no regrets about her married life. But eventually, she'd moved on. Emotionally, when she'd allowed herself to feel again with Jacques, and now she was moving on physically too.

With the packing done and the house cleared, she was exhausted, but ready to leave. She figured she'd have plenty of time to sleep on that dreadfully long flight. There was only one thing left to do, and that was to tell Sam and Kyle about her life-changing decision. She hoped they'd be happy for her, but they could hardly complain.

In the end, she had to leave a message for each of them, which made her a little sorry; she would have liked to explain in person before she left the country. But she comforted herself with the thought that they would phone her as soon as they received the messages, and she might even have some more news for them by then.

* * *

When she arrived in Nice, she was glad she'd booked into a hotel so that she could sleep, and then freshen up before attempting to see Jacques. As it was quite a lot cooler than when she was last there, she dressed in black trousers and a blue sweater that matched her eyes. She thought she looked okay when she looked in the mirror. Not sophisticated or chic, but then Jacques had never seemed to care about that before.

Once she was ready, she considered heading for his villa, but since it was midweek and lunchtime, the restaurant seemed like the better option.

Returning to a place where you'd been happy wasn't always a good idea, she knew. But when she stood on the Promenade des Anglais and turned a full circle, taking in the sights and sounds and smells and everything else she recalled so well, she also knew that, for her, it had been the best idea she'd ever had.

After entering La Bergamote, she took a moment to scan the room before approaching the maître d'.

'Mais, non,' he said when she asked if Jacques was there. He had difficulty hiding his surprise at seeing her, just as she couldn't hide her disappointment when he told her that Jacques had taken some time off.

'I am sorry. He is at home. He has been in a very bad mood for weeks. I believe he did need a holiday.' When he asked if she required a table anyway, she shook her head.

Cheered by the hope that his bad mood might have begun at the time of her leaving, she walked to the old town where she made her way to Jean-Claude's café.

Both Jean-Claude and Chantal, who was now helping behind the counter, gaped at her. When she explained that she'd come back for good, they applauded her decision.

'But does Jacques know about this?' Jean-Claude asked.

'No.' She shook her head. 'Not yet. He's at the vineyard.'

'Ah, but this is not right,' he said, gesticulating. 'You must go to see him there at once. He will want to know.'

'I don't want to intrude.'

He made a sound with his lips that told her what he thought of that statement. 'You must go. He will want to see you.'

'Do you think I should go to see him?' she asked Chantal.

'But of course.' She shrugged. 'That is why you came.'

Well, yes, it was. 'Okay. I'll hire a car and drive myself there.'

She wouldn't have dreamed of driving on the

wrong side of the road when she first came over, but she wasn't afraid of it now. A little wary, yes, but not enough to stop her. She'd changed.

Not expecting her navigational skills to have improved even if she had changed in other ways, she made sure to hire a car with a GPS, *and* bought a road map. Then, with an overnight bag in the car, she set off.

With each kilometre, her stomach tied itself into a tighter knot. By the time she turned into the long driveway with the trees standing to attention on either side, she was feeling sick with nerves, even though she kept telling herself that it would be all right.

Then she saw the house, and it looked welcoming and familiar. Her heart lurched. She'd made it.

She parked at the side of the house as Jacques had done on their earlier visits, then got out of the car and stretched the long drive out of her muscles. The scents of roses and lavender carried to her on the evening breeze, and she smiled at the chirruping of the *cigales*, the Provençal equivalent of Australia's cicadas.

Evening was not the best time to come calling, but she hadn't given a thought to her estimated time of arrival when she'd set out. All she'd been thinking about was seeing Jacques.

She tried to swallow her nervousness as she

walked to the front of the house, but her hand was shaking when she knocked on the door.

Bertrand opened it. He stared, then slowly a smile stretched across his face. 'You've come to put my little brother out of his misery?'

She moistened her lips but could make no sensible response.

'Come in.' He stood aside, but, rather than take her through to one of the rooms she could hear voices emanating from, he indicated the open door of his office. 'Wait in there, please. I will fetch Jacques.' He grinned before closing the door.

She stepped into the room and spared a glance for the large desk piled high with paperwork. Running a winery was not just about making wine, she gathered.

She had her back to the door when she heard it open, and spun around to see Jacques standing right before her. Seeing him again hammered home the significance of what she was doing here.

He looked at her with a contorted face, as if he thought he was going crazy. She'd sprung this meeting on him. Of the two of them, she was the only one prepared for it, but she suddenly didn't feel at all ready.

What had she said about waiting? She had to be kidding. She was so close to having everything she wanted, and she was scared to open her mouth in case she didn't get it. Her heart was beating so hard she couldn't catch her breath. All she could do was stand there, staring.

'Leonie?'

Her knees buckled at the sound of her name on his lips, and she reached for the back of Bertrand's desk chair.

'What are you doing here? Are you okay? Did you forget something?'

On an impulse, she said, 'Yes, I did. I forgot to tell you that I love you.'

His eyes widened. His voice sounded peculiar when he said, 'You read my letter?'

'Yes.'

'And you came back to tell me that?'

'Yes.' She watched him move towards her as if in slow motion. 'And I…' She swallowed. 'I'm going to move back to Nice. For good this time.'

'What about your children?'

'Huh, turns out they're not children anymore.'

His brow furrowed. 'What?'

She sighed. 'They've both moved out of home. They've flown the nest.'

He stepped closer still. 'Are you okay?'

'They don't need me anymore, you see.'

He touched her hair as if he couldn't quite believe she was there. '*I* need you.'

'Oh.' She bit her lip to stop it wobbling, and gave him a shaky smile. 'I don't want to put any pressure on you, Jacques, but I need to know… whether…you want to be with me…long term.'

'More than anything. It's a dream I never dared to have. I couldn't let myself hope because it was never going to happen.' He pushed his fingers into her hair, then tipped her face up for a kiss, and his lips were as warm and firm as she remembered. The kiss went on and on, neither of them wanting to stop, making up for being apart for weeks.

When he finally broke the kiss, they were both panting. And when he said, 'So, will you marry me, my beautiful Leonie?' she simply said,

'Yes.'

They clung to each other for several long moments, then Leonie said, 'But only on one condition.'

She felt Jacques tense, and his eyes narrowed. 'A condition?'

Smiling, she said, 'Only if Antoine will come to live with us at the villa in Nice.'

He laughed and she felt the tension leave him.

'We won't be able to stop him. He's been talking about you ever since you left. We both have.'

She sighed and laid her head against his chest. 'Oh, I've missed you terribly.'

His hold tightened and she sank into him. His arms felt so right, so secure, and she knew: this was her place. She'd found her new home right where she stood. Her future was with him.

EPILOGUE

A YEAR later, Leonie stood at the window of the white-on-white room in the old house, looking out at the magical view of this small part of Provence, with its golden light and gentle way of life.

Jacques' home country. It wasn't hers, but it did hold a very special place in her heart. And it was the perfect place to hold a wedding reception.

A double wedding reception, in fact, because Bertrand and Francine had joined them in marrying at the village church.

Jacques hadn't wanted to wait. He'd been impatient to marry as soon as she'd agreed to be his wife, but one thought had held her back. She'd wanted her children to be present at her wedding, to walk down the aisle with her. She'd wanted Kyle to give her away, and Samantha to be her bridesmaid. She'd wanted them both to give their blessing to her new life with Jacques. She wanted them there to share her happiness.

So, they'd had to wait a year for Sam to return from her stint as an aid worker in Africa. But it had been a wonderful year, full of discovery and joy.

The door opened quietly behind her and she smiled without turning around. She knew it was Jacques. She always knew when he was near. Her husband of one day, but in truth they'd been as good as married for a year already. She turned when she felt his presence behind her.

'Are you ready, my beautiful wife?' he asked, his dark eyes full of adoration. 'People are waiting to eat.'

She nodded. She wouldn't want to come between a Frenchman and his food. That would never do.

Together they descended the stairs and emerged into the courtyard where trestle tables were set up, loaded with baskets of roses and lavender and, naturally, bottles of wine. Guests had spilled from the courtyard into the garden, but the instant they were spotted coming out of the house word spread that it was time to eat and the crowd moved as one to the massive buffet table.

Leonie smothered a grin and scanned the scene for her son and daughter. She found them with Antoine, the three of them chatting and teasing each other like the siblings that they now were. A wave of warmth flowed through her at the sight.

She would always be tied to Australia because Sam and Kyle would make their lives there, but she was needed here. And she was truly happy with Jacques and Antoine, her second-chance family.

ROMANCE 2-in-1

Coming next month

THE GIRL FROM HONEYSUCKLE FARM
by Jessica Steele

Phinn isn't fooled by eligible bachelor Ty's good looks, and sparks fly when she discovers he's the hot-shot London financier who bought her beloved Honeysuckle Farm!

ONE DANCE WITH THE COWBOY
by Donna Alward

Cowboy Drew left Larch Valley promising Jen he'd return. When he didn't, she moved on. Now Drew's back! Could **Cowboys & Confetti** be on the horizon? Find out in the first of a brand-new duet.

THE DAREDEVIL TYCOON
by Barbara McMahon

Escape Around the World. A hot-air balloon race with her daredevil boss, Rafael, is only the beginning of Amalia's Spanish adventure…

HIRED: SASSY ASSISTANT
by Nina Harrington

Medic Kyle has swapped the wilds of Nepal for Lulu's English country house. He wants to publish her famous mother's diaries – that's if he can get this sassy assistant to play ball.

On sale 1st January 2010

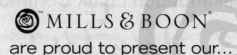

millsandboon.co.uk Community

Join Us!

The Community is the perfect place to meet and chat to kindred spirits who love books and reading as much as you do, but it's also the place to:

- **Get the inside scoop from authors about their latest books**
- **Learn how to write a romance book with advice from our editors**
- **Help us to continue publishing the best in women's fiction**
- **Share your thoughts on the books we publish**
- **Befriend other users**

Forums: Interact with each other as well as authors, editors and a whole host of other users worldwide.

Blogs: Every registered community member has their own blog to tell the world what they're up to and what's on their mind.

Book Challenge: We're aiming to read 5,000 books and have joined forces with The Reading Agency in our inaugural Book Challenge.

Profile Page: Showcase yourself and keep a record of your recent community activity.

Social Networking: We've added buttons at the end of every post to share via digg, Facebook, Google, Yahoo, technorati and de.licio.us.

www.millsandboon.co.uk

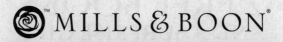

2 FREE BOOKS
AND A SURPRISE GIFT

We would like to take this opportunity to thank you for reading this Mills & Boon® book by offering you the chance to take TWO more specially selected books from the Romance series absolutely FREE! We're also making this offer to introduce you to the benefits of the Mills & Boon® Book Club™—

- **FREE home delivery**
- **FREE gifts and competitions**
- **FREE monthly Newsletter**
- **Exclusive Mills & Boon Book Club offers**
- **Books available before they're in the shops**

Accepting these FREE books and gift places you under no obligation to buy, you may cancel at any time, even after receiving your free shipment. Simply complete your details below and return the entire page to the address below. You don't even need a stamp!

YES Please send me 2 free Romance books and a surprise gift. I understand that unless you hear from me, I will receive 5 superb new stories every month including two 2-in-1 books priced at £4.99 each and a single book priced at £3.19, postage and packing free. I am under no obligation to purchase any books and may cancel my subscription at any time. The free books and gift will be mine to keep in any case.

Ms/Mrs/Miss/Mr_____ Initials _____

Surname _____

Address _____

_____

_____ Postcode _____

Send this whole page to: Mills & Boon Book Club, Free Book Offer, FREEPOST NAT 10298, Richmond, TW9 1BR